SANDRA MUJINGA
SHADOW OF NEW WORLDS

BOM
DIA
BOA
TARDE
BOA
NOITE

Vleeshal

BERGEN KUNSTHALL

Contents

Foreword — 8

Reluctant Celebrity — 18
Wong Bing Hao

S.L.S. — 34
Tamar Clarke-Brown

There's Nothing Black About This — 42
Olamiju Fajemisin

Amnesia? Amnesia? — 82
Jessica Lauren Elizabeth Taylor

Amnesia? Amnesia? — 86
Sandra Mujinga

You Are All You Need — 92
Sandra Mujinga

Re-Imagining Things III — 124
Sandra Mujinga

Colophon — 134

Foreword

This publication accompanies Sandra Mujinga's exhibitions "SONW – Shadow of New Worlds" at Bergen Kunsthall and "Midnight" at Vleeshal, Middelburg. Not strictly a documentation or mediation of these exhibitions, the publication operates rather like a complement to the physical exhibition spaces. It highlights writing and critical discourse as important aspects of Mujinga's artistic practice. Text plays a key role, not only in many of Mujinga's works, but also as a tool to initiate conversations with contributors from various fields of practice. This book contains a selection of Mujinga's scripts for video works and performances, as well as texts by Wong Bing Hao, Tamar Clarke-Brown, Jessica Lauren Elizabeth Taylor, and a conversation with Olamiju Fajemisin. Most of the texts have been written specifically for this publication. Jessica Lauren Elizabeth Taylor's contribution was initially written for Mujinga's exhibition "Amnesia? Amnesia?" at NoPlace in Oslo 2019. The scripts include texts for a video work in the same exhibition, performed by Joe von Hutch, and two performance scores, written for Terese Mungai-Foyn and Mariama Ndure ("You Are All You Need") and Victoria Nunes Finstad and Sanyu Christine Nsubuga ("Re-Imagining Things III"). What connects all of these texts is an interest in collaboration, in a shared conversation about questions that are fundamental for Mujinga's practice, and for which this book provides a platform.

Mujinga uses exhibitions as sites for an adaptable and changeable space, comparable to the way in which a digital image can be subjected to endless edits and changes, without losing its essence. Online one can find Mujinga's sculptures acting in radically different

situations, from illuminated white gallery spaces to darkened stages. The reappearance of works in the exhibitions at Bergen Kunsthall and Vleeshal is thus an integral part of Mujinga's continuous re-staging of artworks. Being aware of the already ubiquitous online presence that art works have today, and her own sculptures and videos in particular, Mujinga chose not to reproduce any images of her own work in the printed book format. Instead, the images in this publication present a specially produced visual essay, conceived as an animation in book form. The images are all stills from footage captured of an elephant outside of Johannesburg, as she moves slowly through the frame of the camera. What the images show, more specifically, are the digitally treated close-ups of the skin of an elephant. The publication's texts are placed within this visual essay, appearing and disappearing throughout the "animated pages" of the book, reflecting on the themes of visibility and invisibility that lie at the core of the two exhibitions in Bergen and Middelburg.

A central work in the two exhibitions is a new hologram video installation titled *Flo* (2019). In this work, a figure with vaguely human features hovers in mid-air in a darkened space without clear boundaries. The protagonist appears like a video game avatar or a science fiction superhero. What may at first glance appear as a digital animation, is in fact one of Mujinga's regular collaborators, the actor and DJ Adrian Blount (GodXXX Noirphiles), dressed in one of the artist's *wearable sculptures*. The hologram technology is frequently used in spectacular stage settings to "resurrect" dead performers or celebrities. Throughout history, new media technologies have often been used in attempts to connect with the afterworld or to revive figures from the past. In this work, named after the artist's mother, technology acts as a bridge between our own world

and an imagined world beyond ourselves, linked to both science fiction and technological performance.

In the two exhibitions, sculptures and videos are seen bathed in a green light, as a filter added to the appearance of the artworks. The green shade of the ambient lighting is reminiscent of the green screen known from video production, where a green background is superimposed with other images, making the relationship between figure and background fundamentally unstable and interchangeable. The black darkness and the green light are opposites, but also two sides of the same coin in Mujinga's work. The green screen functions both as a conceptual and material starting point; a space that can be changed into anything, being nothing and everything simultaneously. The question of what it means to exist in the dark is a recurring topic in Mujinga's practice. The darkness here refers both to invisibility based on hierarchies and exclusion in society, and at the same time to visibility and invisibility in the face of an increasing (and often commercially motivated) surveillance. On the one hand, it is about the productive possibilities for rebellion or peace of mind that invisibility brings—on the other hand, about invisible stories, collective amnesia and about who writes history versus who gets written out and overlooked. Mujinga addresses the heteronormative, largely white hegemony that still dominates the art institution with a questioning and acute awareness, by maintaining the complexity of questions about representation and participation within the same institutional frameworks.

In Mujinga's multidisciplinary practice—from her performances to her active work with public discourse, and from videos and sculptures to her own presence in social media—choosing between being visible and avoiding visibility in full view becomes a productive strategy.

Shadows and darkness transform into a space of agency.
Going under the radar also generates strength.

Axel Wieder and Steinar Sekkingstad, Bergen Kunsthall
Roos Gortzak, Vleeshal

Reluctant Celebrity
Wong Bing Hao

In December 2018, former First Lady of the United States Michelle Obama wore a lemon shirt-dress and gold holographic thigh-high boots, both from Balenciaga, to the concluding public appearance of her book tour for *Becoming*. Fashion critic Robin Givhan exclaimed that "it wasn't just an eye-catching ensemble. It was fashion. Fashion. Faaaashion!" For Givhan, fashion is like a "personal spotlight" that can create a "magnetic" public persona. Providing context for her theatrics, Givhan conjectured that Obama's statement-making style was one of many recent sartorial displays that had, consciously or not, nudged her away from the monolithic conservatism of 'First Lady' toward a more publicly accessible and adulated image. In her sunny, bedazzled Balenciaga, Obama seemed to cast aside previous reservations of the limelight, luxuriating in fashion's celebrity and cultural currency.

Flo (2019), Sandra Mujinga's new artwork that is affectionately named after her mother, is a three-metre-tall hologram modelled after Ann-Marie Crooks, a Jamaican-American former bodybuilder and pro-wrestler. More spooky spectre than fashion glitterati, *Flo* is pictured clad in an elephantine black faux leather suit, and is only visible in momentary flashes throughout the darkened exhibition space. She disappears as soon as she emerges; a different sort of holographic celebrity than Obama. In *Flo*'s brief appearances, her bodily features are scantly identifiable: only a nebulous, skeletal physique can be deciphered. A haunting soundtrack of seraphic string instruments accompanies *Flo*'s temporary intrusions into the exhibition space. Unlike the holograms of deceased celebrities like Tupac and Whitney Houston in popular

revival concerts, *Flo* does not seem to be concerned with the business of preservation, longevity, or self-aggrandisation. Instead, reminiscent of Crooks' enigmatic ring name, Midnight, *Flo* is the virtual embodiment of potent, liminal darkness.

Towering at the same height as *Flo* are seven hooded humanoid sculptures, dispersed through the galleries of Bergen Kunsthall. In several recent exhibitions, Mujinga has experimented with various permutations of these faceless and amorphous giants, playing around with their shapes and proportions, fabric texture and draping, colour, and degrees of exposure. In Tranen, Copenhagen, the alien titans were dressed in structured burgundy trousers which were sliced open to reveal a greyish inner layer. At UKS, Oslo, however, they sported only the flimsier grey fabric that hung eerily around their sparse frames. Sometimes visible are small segments of the clothes' inner linings: a red, pustular material that resembles the brooding behemoths' curdled blood or concealed organs. Mujinga makes this marred "skin" by burning a combination of PVC, glycerine, and a mixture of other plastics and textiles. These imperfect corporeal revelations remind the artist of the trite axiom "wearing your heart on your sleeve," and render the outlandish giants vulnerable, as if they had the capacity to think, feel, and act.[1]

Oddly, at Bergen Kunsthall, Mujinga chose green for this interior flesh. In fact, the entire room is bathed in a green light. Drawing inspiration from science fiction writer Octavia Butler, Mujinga imagines a body that can endlessly shapeshift and camouflage itself, changing colour and form at whim. Instead of its predicable, utopian associations with Nature, why can't green be the colour of bodily flesh? Another point of reference is the

---

1   Skype conversation with the artist, October 2019.

green screen, a representational void that vanquishes all other colours, and therefore a useful backdrop that allows Mujinga to create many of her artworks, including *Flo*. In this case, green, unlike Obama's vivacious sunflower hue, is "the most removed from skin colour." While black is the nihilistic amalgamation of all colours, the green of green screens symbolises pure abstraction, a complete detachment from colour. For Mujinga, black and green are therefore two sides of the same coin; the former overwhelmed by chromatic excess to the point of oblivion, and the latter a metaphorical eraser of colours. By incorporating green into her new sculptures, Mujinga "works with blackness, but not directly."

In her practice, Mujinga tests the representational possibilities of voids and invisibility. A bodybuilder's hard-earned musculature is fragmented and made intangible. Ominous giant portents are surprisingly fragile and emaciated. Green is total emptiness, evacuated of its life-giving associations. In her dissection of European conceptual art exhibitions, cultural theorist Nana Adusei-Poku speculates whether "nothingness ha[s] to be empty, related to white, and, ultimately, be a shrouded representation of whiteness?"[2] Analysing works by transatlantic black artists and thinkers from the 1960s–1990s, Adusei-Poku provokes the assumption of these spaces of art as universal, meditative, and free, by questioning if nothingness can "be foundational for a coming-into-being—a gesture of multiplicity rather than a gesture of absence."[3] In black experiences, the void can be generative, relational, and discursive.

Anthropologist Natalie Newton argues that Saigon's *les*—a local Vietnamese term for 'lesbian'—nurture

---

2   Nana Adusei-Poku, "On Being Present Where You Wish to Disappear." *E-flux 80* (March 2017): https://www.e-flux.com/journal/80/101727/on-being-present-where-you-wish-to-disappear/
3   Ibid.

kinship through what she calls "contingent invisibility." In her ethnography, conducted between 2006 and 2010, Newton observes that *les* community formation is contingent or dependent on overarching civic structures and spaces, which *les* strategically navigate within and repurpose for their benefit. Tactics of anonymity and concealment are perhaps most evident in the *les* concept of "*come out*," a local derivation of "coming out." Unbeknownst to most, on the auspicious day of October 10, 2010 (10–10–10), about 20 *les* cycled down crowded boulevards in downtown Saigon wearing T-shirts in the colours of the pride flag, inaugurating Vietnam's participation in International Coming Out Day (ICOD). Bearing "no explicit signage," and recruiting only a few members by selective invitation, *les* were secretive and "hidden in plain sight . . . challeng[ing] the idea of 'coming out' as a form of public disclosure."[4]

Elsewhere, at a birthday celebration, Newton witnessed birthday girl Bay symbolically propose to her girlfriend on stage with extravagant jewellery while proclaiming her love for her partner. While some *les* cheered on this display of affection, others deemed it "too much," stating that a "true" *les* would never resort to such lurid, ostentatious gimmicks. In contrast to Western norms of "coming out," in the Vietnamese context, "self-disclosure of one's sexuality is not necessarily the ultimate legitimization of *les* sexual subjectivity."[5] Paradoxically, it can undermine the authenticity of *les* subjects.

In liberal discourses, public recognition and spatial occupation are automatically linked to activist

---

[4] Natalie Newton, "Contingent Invisibility: Space, Community, and Invisibility for Les in Saigon." *GLQ: A Journal of Lesbian and Gay Studies* 22, no. 1 (January 2016): 110.

[5] Natalie Newton, "A queer political economy of 'community': Gender, space, and the transnational politics of community for Vietnamese lesbians (*les*) in Saigon" (PhD diss., University of California, Irvine, 2012), 202–4.

'resistance' and 'progress' for queer communities, while invisibility is perceived as a 'deficiency' lacking political intent.[6] Such mutually exclusive binarisations explain the misinformed demonisation of 'Third World' or 'global South' countries like Vietnam as 'backwards' or 'undeveloped' due to a perceived dearth of documented or noticeable queer activity. For ICOD, Saigonese *les* eschewed direct confrontation or opposition to hegemonic social structures, opting instead for degrees of "confidentiality [and] symbolic coding" to protect them from "fears about family rejection, workplace discrimination, and public shaming" on Saigon's busy streets.[7] They were both seen and unseen, conspicuous yet discrete, silently taking a stance; their actions understood only by fellow insiders with whom they bonded in the fleeting moments of public exposure.

Adusei-Poku and Newton's transnational perspectives posit the importance of regional formations and articulations of the self that put a dent in universal claims for 'minority' representation. Their work overhauls socio-political lenses that frame and envision the 'marginal' as necessarily lesser and powerless. Theirs is an ethics of sustainability and self-preservation. Mujinga possesses the same sharp reflexivity in her practice, which unites a wealth of specific resources and communities without placing them at risk of tokenistic involvement.

Illustrative of Mujinga's artistic approach is *Lovely Hosts*, a series of photographs that encircles *Flo* and the extra-terrestrial giants in the exhibition at Bergen Kunsthall. These works were happenstance creations. During a visit to Kisangani, Congo, an employee of a local printing company accidentally destroyed Mujinga's photocard by exposing it to a computer virus. Although

---

6   Newton, "Contingent Invisibility," 114.
7   Newton, "Contingent Invisibility," 110.

her photos were ruined, videos in a travel diary style, taken while commuting in cars throughout Kisangani, were recovered. Taking cues from the viral accident and the apologetic Congolese employee, Mujinga took screen shots of the videos and started developing them as tenderly broken images. As expected, the screen grabs, mainly of people riding on motorbikes, are highly distorted and pixelated. In these photos, bodies and faces are hardly visible, and Kisangani looks like a dystopian cityscape. Mujinga deformed the indiscernible images further by puncturing them with grommets, literally emptying out their contents and making them even harder to read. The prints manifest what Mujinga calls the "physical presence of distortions"; the oxymoron intimating her deft avoidance of touristic, consumptive capture.

Tensions of interpellation extend into the realms of social media applications. Regardless of intent, whether for personal ingratiation or professional promotion, social media activity leaks and infringes on boundaries of being. Disconcerting, certainly, but also opportune; allowing the artist to "exist under her own premise."[8] Unlike, unfollow, hide, mute, block: these are just some functions that allow a user to proactively limit what they deem to be undesirable interaction or attention. Presence can be preserved and controlled. For instance, Mujinga does not follow anyone on Instagram. Reminiscent of the artist's social media reticence is *Coiling*, a new eight-metre-long spiral sculpture marked with the same green, radioactive flesh. At Bergen Kunsthall, it fiercely occupies a corner in a separate exhibition space, appearing just as likely to hiss in recalcitrance at unwanted contact.

8   Skype conversation with the artist, July 2018.

Though seemingly counterintuitive, in Mujinga's thought process, withdrawal on social media apps is an empowering practice. Somewhat similarly, theorist Lisa Nakamura seeks to "rematerialize the Internet," the facilitating technological backbone of social media usage, "by locating its material base in specifically embodied users and producers," especially "socially invisible bodies."[9] Nakamura and other scholars debunk utopian assumptions of the Internet as a level playing field where cultural particularities do not matter. Mujinga pushes this social campaign further by questioning its necessity. Throughout her practice, she asks: What constitutes social visibility? Does one even *need* to be seen? Mujinga's formalist deployments offer nuanced responses to these important questions, leading optimists down a pitch-dark cul-de-sac.

9   Lisa Nakamura, *Digitizing Race: Visual Cultures of the Internet* (Minneapolis: University of Minnesota Press, 2007), 203.

S.L.S.
Tamar Clarke-Brown

'It's going to take a while,'
they said,
'to make this silver-lining suit,
thread salvaged
from the
skirting of black holes . . . '
•
but even when there was no sun
I wanted to stay a little longer
find time to pack my bags
and cast
a gibbous form
from sunken rays

And so
impatient,
I multiplied my moons
and found another source
built a scaffold to my dimple
and sunk a line into its cache
watched its shadow mas -
and turn up silver linings
in its echoes.

Casting outwards and around
avoiding the dimple's centre
I started to collect matter from its contours
all the stuff around the edges
of its event horizon.

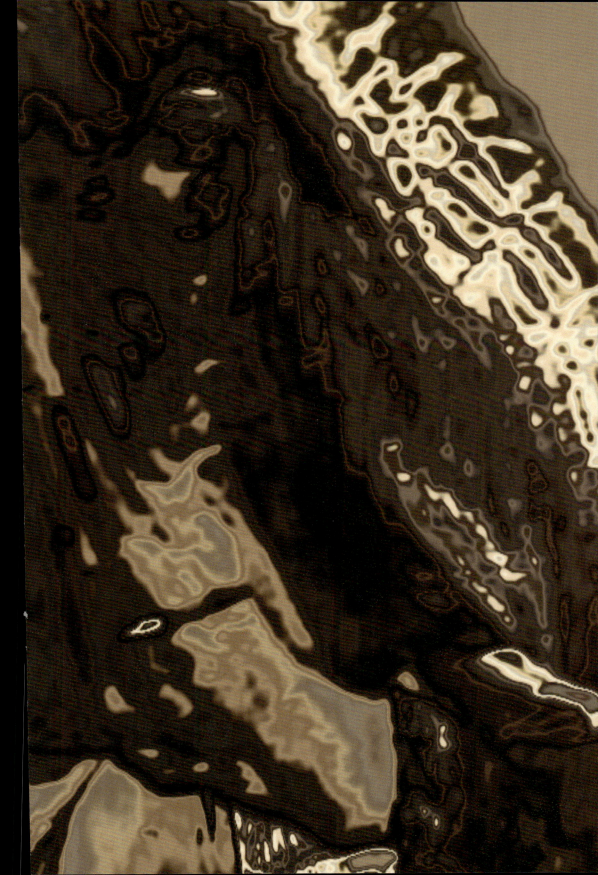

I was catching
and so
I cast another line
and then another
stretched out my fingers
and played cat's cradle
above nature's reserve:
a consenting excavation.

Some time spent fishing
turning up
the remnants of soft fictions
and reworked memories keeping me in orbit.

I leaned back
pulling the lines of my fingers taut
to recover the last;
a stretched-out psyche
of melanistic matter,
like Senga Nengudi tights.

I reeled it all in
and started to sew
at some point after midnight.
A silver-lining suit
of max tensile strength
and made from my own shadow's mass.
•

Cycle forward.
Some time spent swimming and I shrug off this suiting
now a baggy primer,
a languid silhouette.
I roll it down
around my ankles
and step out
let it pool on the floor
and perform its own eclipse.

Then
I
cast my line
into its andisol
tread the perimeter
and curve around its edges,
collecting the dust
to spin another
a silver-lining suit
for times of limbo.

•
the first stretches of
a slow elaboration
called
moonlighting as my shadow
•

A retrograde orogeny.

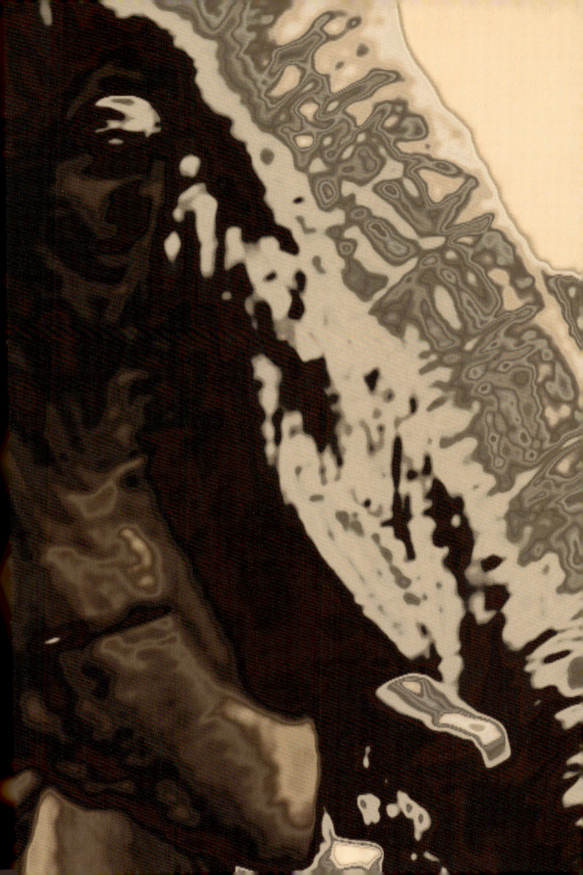

There's Nothing Black About This
Olamiju Fajemisin

Sandra Mujinga   What were we talking about?

Olamiju Fajemisin   Violent spaces.

SM   Sometimes you have to go through these spaces.

OF   Of course, not everyone has the means to carve out their own. You might not have that community around you. It was relatively easy—and I don't use that term lightly—for collectives like BBZ, Pxssy Palace, *gal-dem* to form because there was a community, a demographic to cater to in London. There were a lot of people living in the same place, both willing and able to put in the work. I've never been to Scandinavia, but I can imagine that there's not as much opportunity for People of Colour, especially Black women to find that community, form collectives...

SM   It's quite interesting, what we were talking about earlier. Being "aware" that you are Black, that you are visible in a certain way. It's something that recurs again and again in my work. I've been thinking a lot about feedback loops, and call-and-response—social media has helped me with that in a way. I can "meet" with other black women through following hashtags. You don't feel so alone.

OF   It provides a sense of relief and comradery, and I'm grateful to social media for that. It definitely helped me find my Black woman friends, here in Berlin.

SM   That's the first step. Like with us, for example, we communicated via Instagram, which then translated into

other spaces. It's a mixture, for me. In the beginning, I felt a sense of responsibility as an educator, but at the same time, I really wanted to re-imagine something, to seek alternative narratives and stories.

OF   What you just said, about responsibility. Super interesting. Responsibility can be quite exhausting. For me, it's been a lot of saying "no" to things because it's tiring having to explain certain concepts over and over; granted, for me they are self-explanatory. But, just because I happen to be Black, and I happen to write, doesn't mean that I hope to be sequestered to the corner of "Black Writer".

There's been a lot of interesting work put out in recent years, though in my opinion, a lot of it seems to pander to what is an inevitably white audience. Think about who can go to galleries in Berlin, New York, Oslo, London, as a form of leisure. It's a privileged sphere. I feel that some people have had to sacrifice the integrity of their intention for the sake of the audience's feelings. Like the new Kara Walker sculpture at Tate Modern, *Fons Americanus* (2019), which attempts to critique London's colonial relics and monuments thorough the placement of an oversized, explicitly decorated, and narratively satirical fountain in Tate Modern's Turbine Hall. Water gushes from the open wound on the reimagined Venus's neck. The figure of a man, a slave I assume, sports goggles as he swims away from a toothy shark. The double-endedness found in this work is not dissimilar to those found in *A Subtlety* (2014), they are quite camp. To have something of that calibre at Tate is in many ways unprecedented, but we need to speak immediately. There was no supplementary material discussing the history of Tate itself. Nothing relating the history of the institution to the context of Walker's work, though they are inextricably linked. Neither Tate, nor Tate & Lyle

sugar. There was no acknowledgement of the colonial skeleton that still supports that institution. I found that really disappointing . . . I fear the installation will be remembered for what it failed to achieve as a supposedly decolonial artwork.

SM   It goes back to white guilt. It's a mindfuck. There are so many layers. I keep thinking about this Black Mirror episode, the one with Daniel Kaluuya. What happens is that they're contestants and they perform to an audience, for points. All of a sudden, Daniel's colleague disappears—or something happens—and he tries to get her back. So instead of following the routine, he says: "I'm gonna do something extreme! I'm gonna smash the window!" The window separates him from the audience. "I'll take a piece of glass and hold it up towards my throat." He planned to say: "If you don't tell me where my colleague is, I'll cut myself!" So, then, in the next scene, you see him waking up in a really nice apartment and he walks towards this—I don't know—window or door, and then he opens it and says: "Yeah, I'm ready." Then he says again: "If you don't tell me where my colleague is, I'll cut myself!" The audience starts clapping and cheering. It became an act. His "act" incorporates itself within the machine. That's what I mean. How critical you are as an artist can become a part of the structure you're trying to challenge. At the beginning, you see what he's doing as an act of self-sacrificial rebellion. This is how he can get his friend back! But then, it's just subsumed. The producers praise him; give him feedback.

OF   It's like the commodification of trauma.

SM   Exactly.

OF   And martyrdom. And radicality. I've never seen that episode. I'm definitely going to watch it.

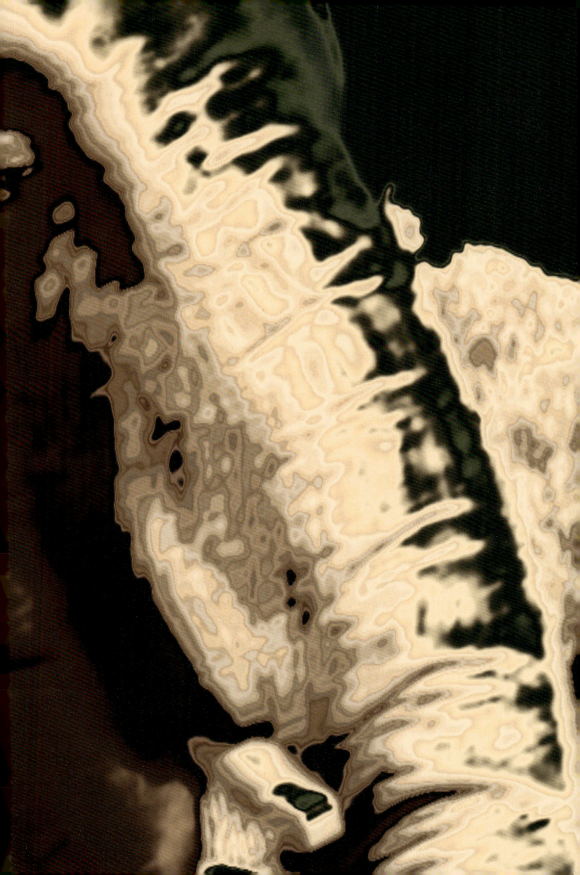

SM   With regard to Black pain, and Black trauma: when I see artists, Black artists using this in their work, displaying that, I, as a Black person, feel traumatised. Then I look to the side and see a white audience Instagramming, taking selfies in front of this image of total violence.

OF   The only exhibition I've been to, recently, where I didn't feel that porn-consuming gaze from the white audience was the Arthur Jafa show at the Julia Stoschek Collection. That made for truly uncomfortable viewing. It definitely played into the use of shock-value imagery, but I felt that it was incredibly honest. It was incredibly candid. I didn't feel that people were fascinated by the trauma of it all. It was more matter-of-fact. I was deeply moved and afterwards thought a lot about the inextricable link between Black joy and suffering. It's hard to make a show about Black identity—about person and experience—that doesn't "perform". Like Diamond Stingily's show in Munich at the Kunstverein—I was there recently. That was really good.

SM   I really liked her show at Galerie Isabella Bortolozzi.

OF   That was great, the Kanekalon hair and what she was using it for. The pieces in Munich were really special. It was about collective memory and nostalgia, not "explicit" Blackness. Yet some of the reviews that came out the morning after it opened wanted to talk about violence in Chicago and so on. It had nothing to do with the work. I mean . . . her show was about childhood! About nostalgia! Perhaps it seemed ridiculous that an artist who happens to be a woman and happens to be Black could make work on her own terms.

Do you feel it's an unfair burden? Isn't there beauty in knowing you mustn't fear that people won't "get it"? "How am I going to explain this to people who haven't

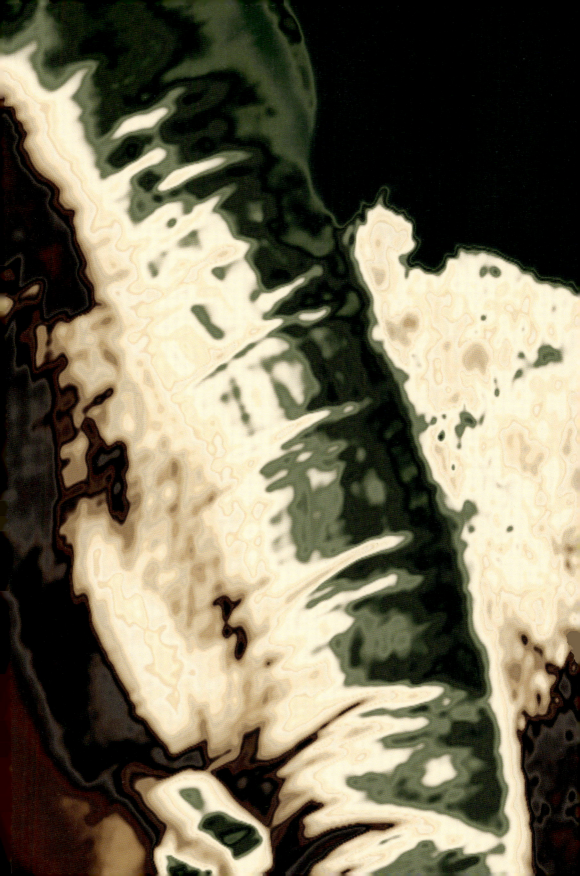

experienced what I have experienced?" Anyway, the topics you deal with in the show—visibility, invisibility, absence—made me think about the way people describe black as an "absence" of colour and light.

SM   And it's the opposite.

OF   Yes, I agree. I think I'm very light, and colourful. When talking about Blackness in art, and literature, and everything else, how do you relate to the definition of Blackness as being an "absence of"?

SM   It's what I'm trying to deal with through my work. I'm interested in understanding "Black" as the combination of all colours as well as the total absence of colour. It's why I've been working with a lot of green screen recently. I've used it for a long time, and it's "black" for me.

OF   It's your starting point.

SM   Yeah! In my videos, when you see a black background, it's green screen. It allows me to host ideas and alternative spaces. Green is ultimately Black. Especially in my recent work, I've been dealing heavily with Blackness in relation to melanin and colourism, and thinking through this in relation to the sun. Thinking about how I grew up with family members telling me to hide from the sun so as not to become darker. You become very aware of how the sun is continually changing, the skin of the earth is getting thinner. It's interesting to then draw it all together. The sun is a brutal God.

OF   Is that what led you to think of visibility and invisibility as survival mechanisms? As means of protecting oneself?

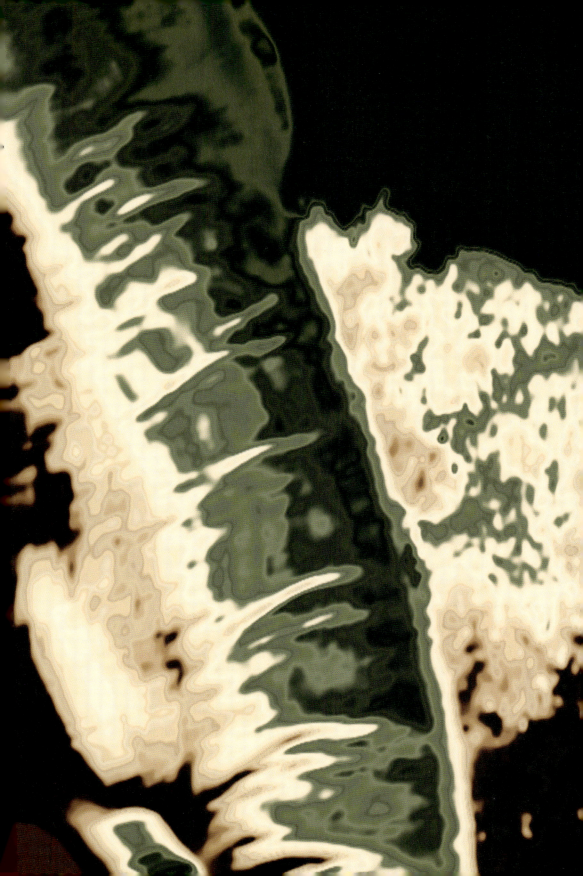

SM   I'm always going back and forth. When I think in terms of visibility, I'm thinking about representation, performance, and theatre.

OF   Being hypervisible?

SM   Hypervisible. People say we're doing great, okay, just because there are darker-skinned supermodels, Black people speaking on panels . . . it's a showcase. It goes back to what we were talking about earlier, what are these spaces we're being invited into? How free are we? I started thinking, what if it does the opposite? I'm super aware of going to exhibitions, being photographed.

OF   I know someone—I don't want to name-drop—a Black journalist who lives in London, who noticed that she and a friend of hers, also Black, were being photographed by a big-name photographer at Kara's opening at Tate, in front of the fountain. As if they were ornamental.

SM   There's power in inclusion, but are we really in control of our narratives? Are you really in charge of how you're being presented? Maybe not.

OF   How else can we be in charge of how we're represented unless we build the platforms of representation ourselves? I was thinking about this earlier this year, in relation to Black Cyberfeminism, and how it's kind of doomed to fail. Not to sound like a total pessimist, but, it's going to be almost impossible to carve out a healthy, functional space for Black feminist discourse on a platform, the Internet, which was built without us in mind. There are Facebook groups and email chains and Tumblr threads, but they're prone to being shut down, or censored, or reported, or trolled. So much free labour. At times it feels futile and it makes me wonder: can

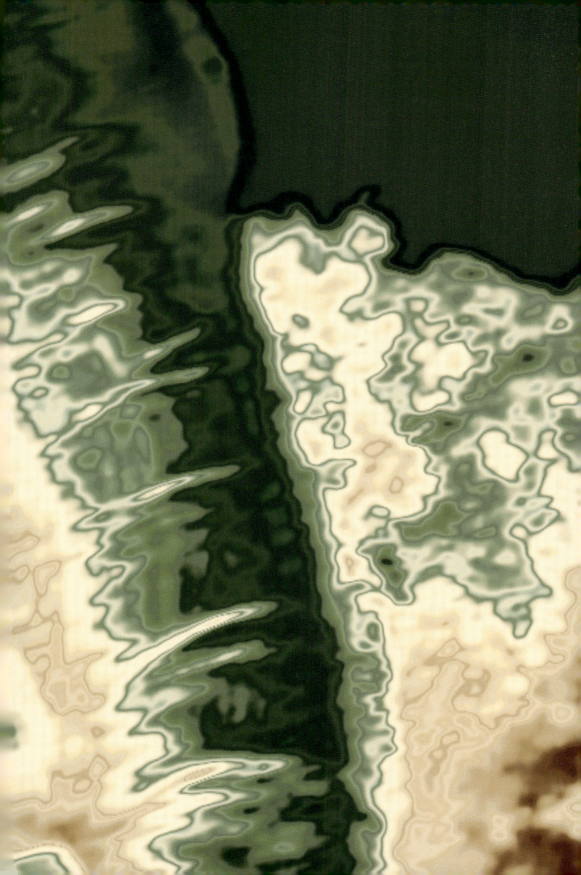

digital Black utopia exist without the creation of a New Internet?

SM   Being online greatly affects my work. It's why I started doing performances where my models and actors are all in the dark, for instance. The longer you're in a space that was completely dark when you entered it, the easier it is to walk and manoeuvre. Your eyes adjust. When trying to create alternate, digital realities, we must reckon with those who have already "adjusted". We end up working for other people, or run the risk of being shut down, or appropriated from. I hear that again and again from Black women.

OF   I love @diet_prada for that.

SM   Me too!

OF   I really do! It is upsetting seeing just how many Women of Colour are having their work ripped-off.

SM   Yeah, now we can fight it, call people out.

OF   Social apocalypse.

•

SM   Sometimes, I feel that I'm too dark, my mind.

OF   Have you ever considered using Vantablack?

SM   What's that?

OF   A material, I think. Subatomically bonded carbon or something. It's the darkest substance on earth. Man-made. It's the complete and total absence of colour. In videos, it appears as a perfect glitch on the screen, like

a cut-out, as if there's nothing there. If someone holds a piece of it, it looks like a void on their palm. If you take a picture of it—even with flash—it will just absorb the light, reflecting nothing. It's the darkest substance—or matter—ever. I think Anish Kapoor bought the rights to use it artistically. Then in retaliation, another artist created the bluest blue, or pinkest pink, or something, then forbade Anish Kapoor from ever using it. It became this whole thing. Anyway, when I was thinking about visibility, invisibility, I thought about Vantablack. In its essence, it is invisible. It cannot be "seen". By definition, you "see" something when light reflects off an object, then into your eyes, right? But if there's no light to be reflected, are we even seeing it?

SM   Kind of like a surveillance issue. Wasn't he just outbid for another colour or something?

OF   Probably, I don't know. I guess I just read half the article.

SM   I'm drawn to the idea though. Just absorbing, not reflecting. Not reflecting back. I think of it in terms of continually bouncing things back. When light hits an object, then it reflects back, then back again . . . it's almost like labour.

OF   It's exhausting. I wonder how relaxing it would be to never be seen.

SM   Just absorbing. This idea of constantly reflecting and mirroring one's surroundings is ultimately tied to survival. You don't want to give anything back! Just absorb.

OF   Absorb and assimilate.

SM   Exhausting, yes. All this time and labour to exist, simply.

OF   This concept stood out in the material you sent me: "The economies and values of disappearance." What is the value of disappearance to you?

SM   [sighs, pointedly]

OF   A chance to exhale, just like that?

SM   Exactly! I joke a lot with my friends about the idea of disappearing in the forest. I went to a Swedish art academy where students used to talk about going to the forest. All the time.

OF   To do what?

SM   They were tired. I thought of it as a privilege. A person must have a certain amount of cultural capital to say that they just want to disappear, and can.

OF   The privilege of relaxation, the price of it.

SM   Even though I'm talking about hiding, disappearance, I'm very much aware of this privilege. Having to represent something, visibly; being visible in such a way so that you can disappear! Like what Hito Steyerl was saying, about having fifteen minutes of not being visible.

OF   Does this play into your interests in science fiction, and elephants? People deciding that they want to be nocturnal?

SM   It comes into my science fiction, yes. It gives me the space to say: "This person is a jellyfish . . . but also has

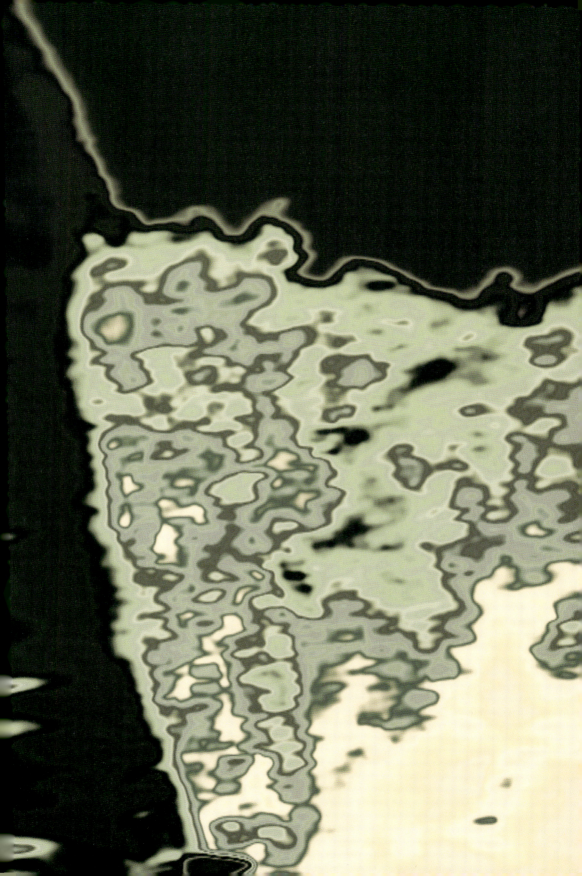

the skin of an elephant, sometimes". Borrowing traits from other species.

OF   Moving away from anthropocentrism.

SM   Exactly.

OF   Moving away from human expectation?

SM   Yes. I like the unexpected. There's something powerful about how we can never really fully understand the characters that I build. There's a shift. In regard to representational politics, it's never only about being "visible" or "representative" of something. There's already an expectation of the Black body, so it's more interesting when you meet people who are just ... *changing*.

OF   And subverting that expectation. And I think that's exactly what you're doing with this show! Because there is an expectation as to the calibre of work a Black artist should produce. There's a lot of talk of "darkness" and "Blackness" in the press release, but then when people actually go and see the show, they'll see the many manifestations of those terms at your hand.

SM   Shapeshifting is of interest too.

OF   Shapeshifting, yes, you also wrote to me about changes of identity through migration.

SM   Not standing still. It is a very general term; I'm being more specific with it.

OF   Human migration?

SM   Yes.

OF   Economic migration.

SM   Specifically. At the beginning of my practice, I spent so much time concerned with how Blackness and my work worked together. I'd say, "there's nothing Black about this!"

OF   "There's nothing Black about this!" What a line.

SM   Now I'm like: "You know what! I can say, 'Black', 'Blackness', 'Migration', whatever, if I want, and *maybe*, it means something else!"

OF   It's on your own terms.

SM   There are all these different strategies to being free. I ask myself all the time: when are you really free?

OF   Is that the strategy with which you free yourself? By... I don't want to say, "redefining these words", because the definition hasn't changed, it's just the context to which they're applied, and your confidence. This has happened with so many words, like "immigrant" and "expat".

SM   People already have a specific person, body in mind when those words are used.

OF   It's telling.

SM   Telling yes, and important to reveal. It's important to allow words the space to reveal themselves. It's interesting, going through phases of not working with certain words. I restrict myself, because I think that will free me to make art about exactly what I want.

•

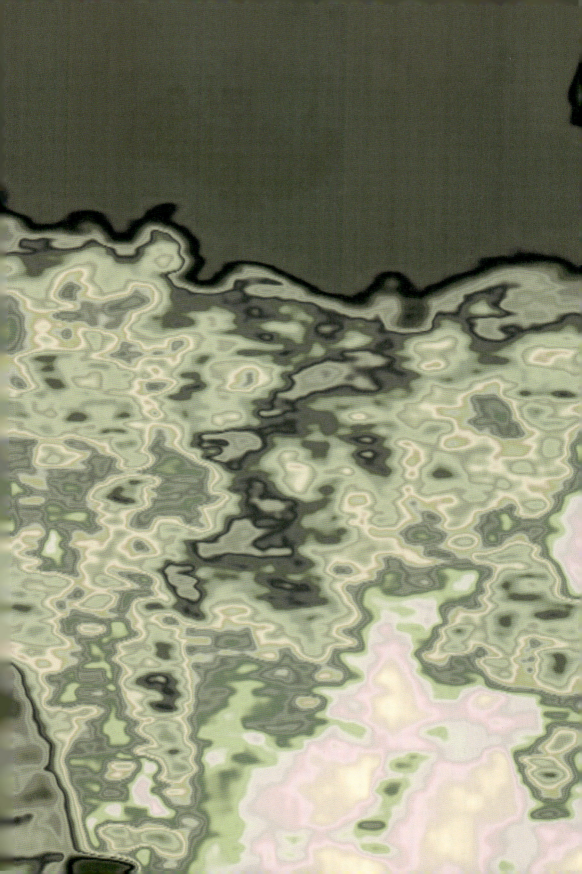

OF   To revisit these ideas: light, dark, invisibility, visibility, colour and the absence thereof. What about shadows?

SM   Totally. I love thinking about them. I watch shadow theatre shows on YouTube.

OF   Never seen any of them!

SM   Oh, it's so awkward. There's a group of people behind fabric, and there's music playing, and they'll sing and create shapes out of their bodies, like stars. Then they're a car. Then they're something else and everyone's like, "Oh, wow! How amazing! How beautiful! How powerful!"

They always end up forming the shape of a heart. Anyway, I'm so drawn to it. To the idea of it. I think it's funny to look at it. This idea that you have something so clearly in front of you, and it gives you space in its not being totally visible. Then using the light to create these illusions, to shapeshift. I'm *very* drawn to it.

OF   It's the only human way we can shapeshift. Or be taught to. Do you remember making rabbit ears with your fingers? When I think of shadow theatre, I remember being a kid, and going to shows where the performers manipulated the size of their bodies by moving closer towards and further away from the light source. They manipulated their presence and the way they existed in that space, through illusion! Kind of like the Platonian world of the forms. Genius and shadows and the manipulation of truth. "In order to have real knowledge, we must gain it through philosophical reasoning." It's interesting how comforting shadows can be, and how much control we have over them. We can project exactly what we want to be seen.

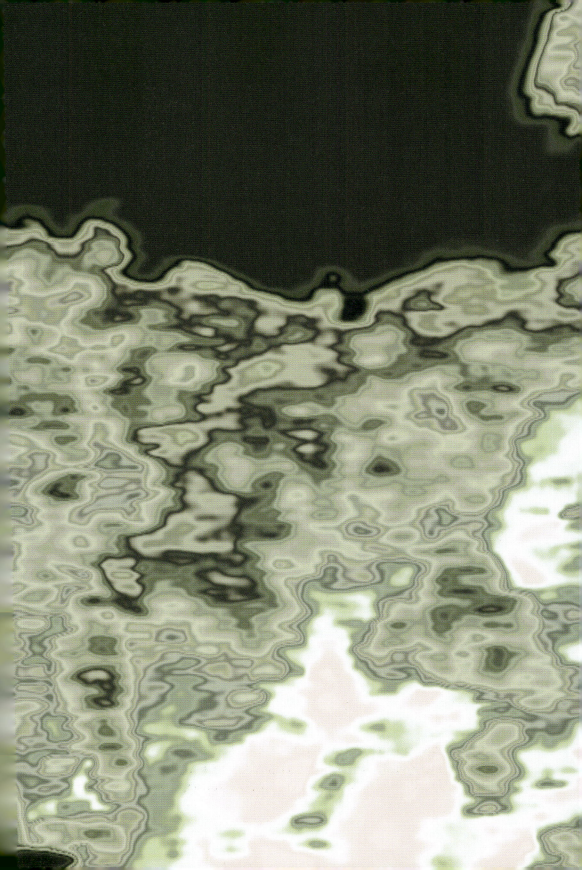

SM   I deal with the manipulation of light, with the projectors in this exhibition. It's been a nice way to think about my work, and the way I make my sculptures for instance. I often imagine that if there was light cast onto them, they would look abstract, but then when you see them as shadows, it would look like an elephant. I find it interesting, what you mentioned, about shadows and light and distance. The further you are from the light, the smaller the shadow is. The more light on you, or an object, the smaller you, or it, "feels".

OF   That's what we were saying earlier about visibility and invisibility, and how relaxing it was for you when you spent part of your childhood in Kenya. For me, this was my childhood summers in Lagos, just being surrounded by people that looked like me, us. Not having to be so conscious about the fact of my visibility. We could just exist. The more hypervisible a person, the more pressure there is for them to be an example.

SM   For me, part of the comfort of shadows comes from giving myself permission to use them as a strategy. When thinking of science fiction, and some may look at this as escapist, but I see shadows as a framework within which to reimagine other bodies.

OF   It's almost like we need to create alternate realities against which we can compare our own. I'm trying to think of a science fiction film I've seen lately that I enjoyed, but I can't even think of one.

SM   Well, it's mainly books.

OF   Yes, science fiction books, more so than fantasy. Science fiction exists within the realm of possibility. I love space films. I want to see the new Brad Pitt one.

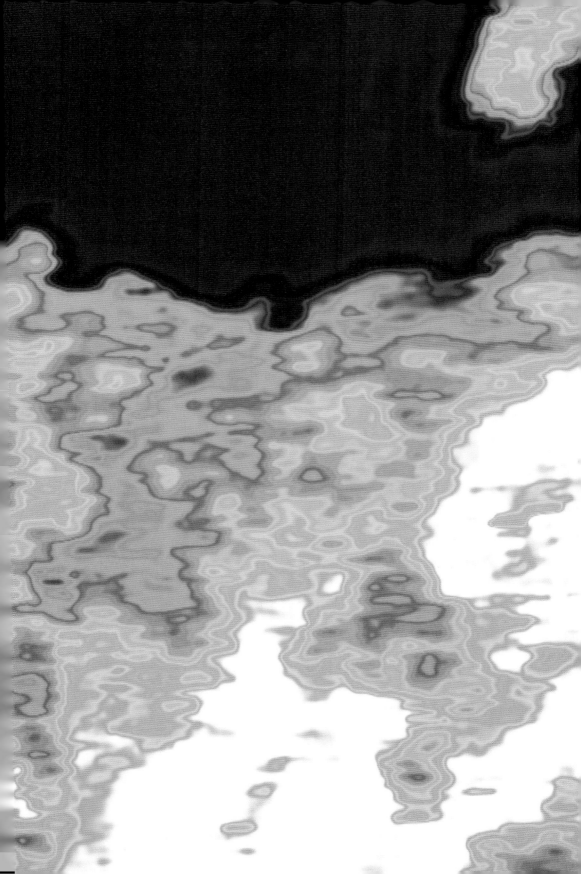

They go to Mars, stopping off at the moon, like it's a terminal to enter the rest of space.

SM   Did you see the Sandra Bullock one?

OF   I watched it like last week.

SM   But you didn't see it in the cinema.

OF   I did too!

SM   I saw it in 3D.

OF   Same. Did you like it?

SM   ... yeah. I liked it, but I don't remember it so much. I just remember this song, this world music type song at the end, when she arrived, or landed.

OF   World music?

SM   Yes!

OF   The film is just her screaming, to be honest.

SM   What's the name of that guy? Blake Lively's husband?

OF   Ryan Reynolds.

SM   Have you seen his film *Buried*?

OF   No I didn't.

SM   I think it's more interesting.

OF   Oh yeah, what's it about?

SM   He's just buried.

OF   Oh.

SM   He's in a box.

OF   Okay.

SM   Underground.

OF   Underground.

SM   He wakes up and . . . I found it more interesting because of where the camera was placed. It made for claustrophobic viewing.

OF   Is it on Netflix?

SM   I don't think so.

OF   I'll find a way.

SM   Yeah. Somehow I associate it with space films. Confined space.

OF   Surveying the human condition in extreme conditions. Under a lot of pressure.

SM   Psychological. But why is it always the lost father figure? "I have daddy issues. I'll solve my issues, and save the world."

OF   Two birds, one stone. Thinking about science fiction. I'm so sure I'll always answer the question, "what would your superpower be?" with invisibility.

SM   Yes.

OF   I think my mum always used to say that she'd fly. But there's so much power in choosing when and where you can be seen, and by whom.

SM   I'd choose that too. Also self-cloning.

OF   That's like, the ultimate hypervisible situation.

SM   It is. Twenty versions of myself. One is in London, the others are in . . . wherever. Again, giving yourself freedom through having . . . twenty bodies.

OF   What would you do if you were invisible for a day? I'd sneak around. Break in somewhere maybe.

SM   Yeah but wouldn't you think that you shouldn't be seeing whatever it is that you're seeing?

OF   But isn't that the joy of it?

SM   I think I'd be too shy.

OF   I would take the piss.

SM   I'd do things for myself. You know . . . okay maybe I would steal stuff.

OF   Rob a bank? It would be rude not to.

SM   Snatch all the Air Jordans.

OF   I want a Telfar bag. Like yours!

•

SM   Sometimes, when I'm writing, I have a need for a space in which things are not clear. I can work with

characters that are arguing, but it's not clear why they're arguing. It's not a means of censoring myself, rather investigating myself, rendering invisibility in words. What do you think when it comes to working with text?

OF   It's a way of protecting yourself, not giving everything, whether it's a character or autobiography. A lack of transparency acts as a shield. I enjoy films where we don't know a character's name, or a vital piece of backstory. I enjoy the anonymity. I was taught to give up everything in the first paragraph. "Hi! I'm blah blah blah, I'm this-many-years-old, I live here, and these are my favourite things. I was born on this day at this time and I'm a Cancer." Why?

SM   It makes me think of that recent Frank Ocean interview. For *GQ* or something. He talks about the power of lies, and how it's so expected of a person, an artist, to always "speak your truth". He talks about how tiring and difficult it is to maintain this.

OF   But when has art ever been about candor and truth? It's always been the appropriation of one story into another, manipulating ideas in accordance with aesthetics, but was it ever intended to be one-hundred-percent honest? I don't think it should be. I love Frank Ocean. His appeal is in the mystery, right? There's a public entitlement to people, public figures. Artists, musicians and writers. There's an idea that if people are willing to be creative, they must also be willing to give up every last thought.

SM   It's why I'm drawn to how Rihanna represents herself. She's her own muse and the face of her own product.

OF   It's very calculated.

SM   Yes very calculated and very specific. Even in my own case, I use social media to be "visible" so I don't have to be "visible" otherwise. It's funny because, sometimes people—who have only just met me but have seen one of my selfies—feel as if they know me.

OF   With everything being so public these days, it's quite powerful to keep things to oneself. This is the first time we've spent time together, though we've been in Insta-contact. I guess I had an idea of what you'd be like.

SM   And how does it compare?

OF   [laughs] Well . . .

SM   Do you think I'm too revealing?

OF   No, not at all. I follow plenty of people, simply for the mess of it all.

SM   What you'll notice on my feed is that it's mostly selfies. Everything kind of happens in my stories. I like to keep tabs on who's watching.

OF   Honestly, same.

SM   I can shapeshift with my selfies, it's a mask, but when it comes to things I'm interested in, that inspire my work, music, I put it all on stories. You know what, a friend gave me a really nice compliment. They said that every time I post a song, it's like I'm introducing a friend!

OF   That's a nice thing to say. What kind of music do you listen to?

SM   Everything. Black metal. Today was Burna Boy. But when I DJ, I play other stuff, like DJ Arafat,

Coupé-Décalé. It gives me this energy, this like [grits teeth and grunts] energy! After that, it gets too much, and I'll listen to some Summer Walker.

Amnesia? Amnesia?
Jessica Lauren Elizabeth Taylor

They say amnesia is rare, but I think we forget all the time.

Don't crawl on your knees.
I forgot.
Stay out of the sun.
I forgot.
You're getting too dark.
I forgot.

Who is privileged enough to forget and who is tasked to remember? Skin slathered in coconut oil laid out on psychedelic beach towels. Search: "How to Turn a Sunburn into a Tan". Bright red skin blistering in the sun, boils popped and soothed with aloe, peeled skin reveals a shiny light brown (not TOO brown) complexion. All of the suffering has been worth it. The pain is forgotten.

The ones who remember have the pain etched in their (OUR) bones. The ones tasked with being too dark for this world take on an assignment they never asked for: to force themselves to remember while continuously being asked to forget. Search: "How to Unlearn Self-Hatred". Grandmas, aunties and play cousins reinforce the internal struggle with creams, shaded partitions and idioms hell bent on squashing out the bright light that comes from being dark. If darkness is a void, then Blackness is a cosmic void: abundant implosions of visionary energy as a direct result of systemic compression.

Amnesia? Amnesia?
Sandra Mujinga

At the moment it really doesn't matter how you ended up here.

It is said that we tend to forget the dark, we also tend to move towards the dark. What do I mean by dark, the dark, the absence of light.

You might feel something but cannot see it.

What you feel should also have the right to bite you.

We forget the dark, darkness, there is too much darkness out there, and if it's uncomfortable it is best for us to forget it.

Am I too dark?

Ok, I am not sending you light. I want you to stay here with me in the dark.

The album is really powerful, he is so vulnerable, and he begs his x not to leave. The album is celebrated by everyone.

I like it too. There is also this part of me that is like . . . what if he's just fucking stalking her, and she just wants to be left alone, and now the whole world is stalking her too, not letting her go.

I have been advised against the dark, it gets you nowhere.

We forgot what led to the break-up—we are all begging her to take him back. To take a chance. Right?

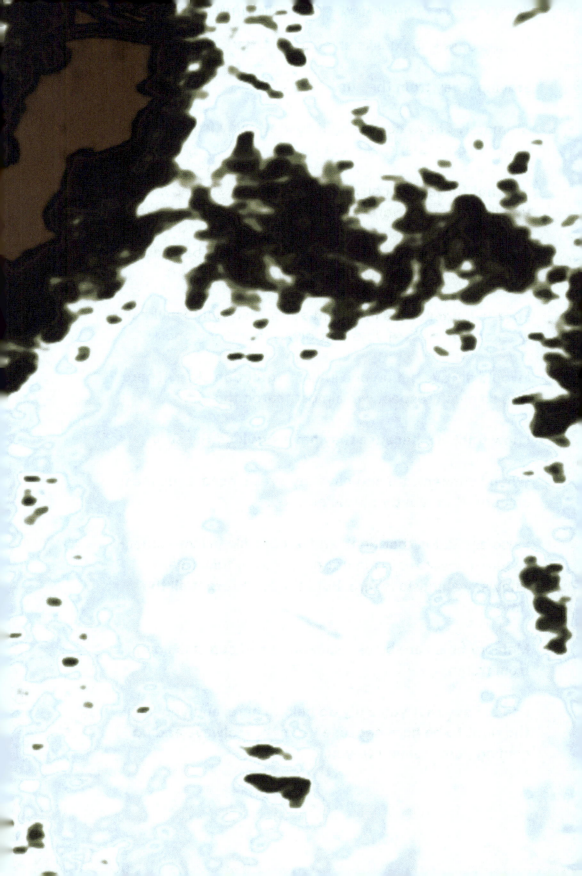

Having dark knuckles is an aesthetic, dark rashes too.

Staying away from the sun.

Ultimately I have been taught to stay away from the sun, to not become darkness itself.

I did not forget our conversation, I simply started a new timeline. In other words, I wish you followed me instead.

Why do we tend to forget what is bad for us, bad habits they call it, but I also call it pressure.

For the longest time I thought sunscreen would make me weaker, but I was always just given the wrong one.

I would always get on one knee, to greet an elder. There was so much respect, we almost feared the old.

I now think it's because they have survived the sun.

When I concentrate and have my eyes closed, I see many colours—but mostly purple and red.

I also see fluids that float, and it looks like a live-screen-saver—except that I am not prepared to fully relax. They say amnesia is rare, but I think we forget all the time.

Memory holes are black, blackouts, and can also come from trauma.

I do believe that you truly do belong here, and you have the right to be here because I somehow always end up coming here, coming to you.

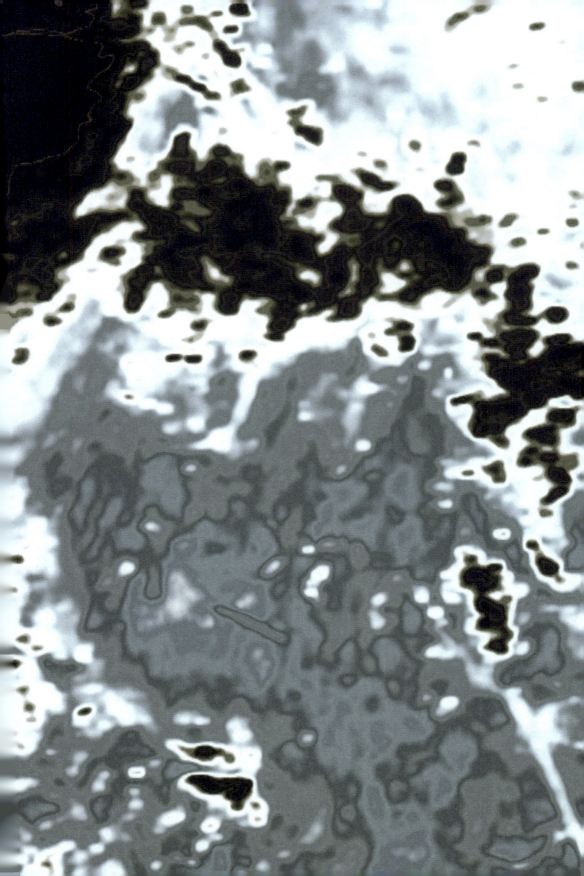

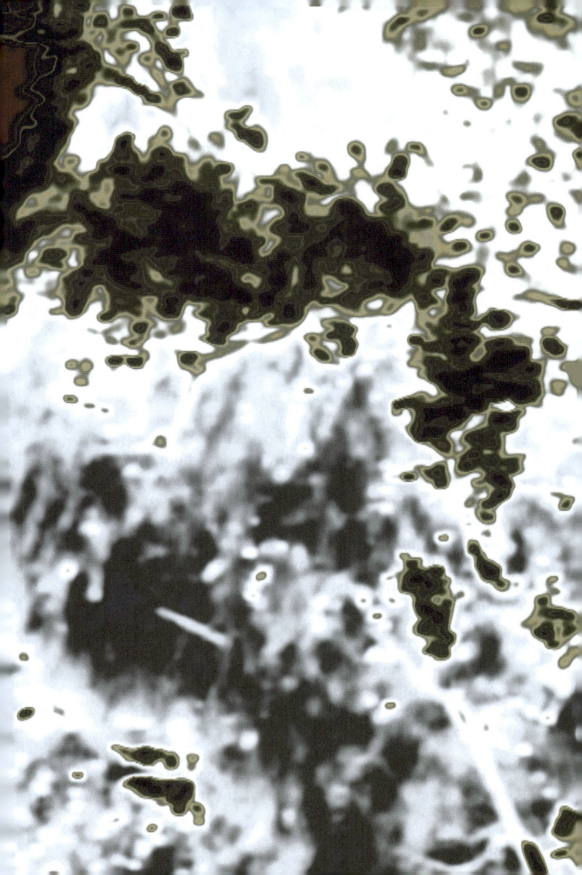

You Are All You Need
Sandra Mujinga

Solo Nkama   My name is Solo Nkama, I am based in Mamugh. For the longest time I have worked with moving images but now I primarily work with text. I will talk more about this later...

I teach at Ehnjatenjate art school, and besides that, I like expanding my practice through working with other artists, I also curate shows and write for Wodmosam Magazine. A couple of years ago I curated a group show titled "You Are All You Need" in Ngogobeihli and I am currently working on a show that will open in a couple of months in Mamugh.

Tala Zomi   My name is Tala Zomi, I am an artist based in Ngogobeihli. I am primarily a sculptor and I also use text in my work. I started producing work that was inspired by closure, or thinking through and about closure. After what happened in Ngogobeihli, there was generally an interest in working through... and mourning the event by having exhibitions. I like to materialise my ideas through working with text, text as something physical—letters having a start and an end in themselves. Recently I have been working with books and publishing.

I, like many artists, spend a lot of time thinking about what it means to be an artist, or what it would be like for me. One of these overall methods I find interesting is hosting distortions. Doing that enabled me to generally take more risks.

What I find striking about your work is self-annihilation...? For the longest time video was seen as the medium that

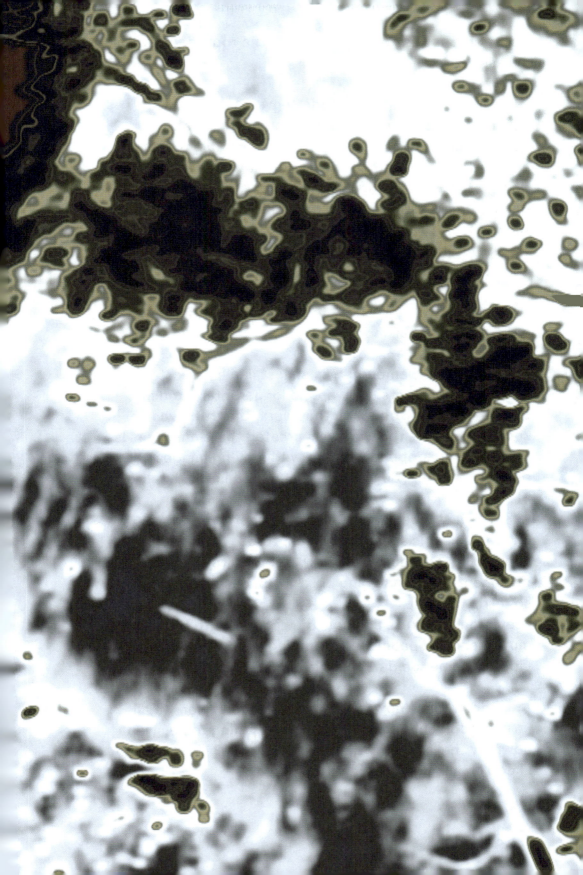

would surpass us, having objects in the room seemed excessive.

SN   I remember the artist Didi Ongwanashi would basically exhibit their editing material, open, and whoever came to the exhibition would be able to edit and even delete parts of the work that was there or do so later when they got home . . . So the work was being produced there and then and maybe, always just temporary? It seemed cheesy at the time, but the work was never meant to be finished. A work had to happen in a limited amount of time, and "disappear".

It was like we all agreed that video told lies, and the artist did not want to tell more lies.

TZ   Right? I remember it was almost like a panic, that unlike our ancestors, we were no longer interested in documenting a truth? With that work, the truth was not something fixed, the work was created there and then. Is that why you stopped working with moving images? You needed a truth? You were tired of telling lies?

SN   The last video I made was very short, very rich, like the volcanic soil it tried to capture . . . Still not convincing, or it does not show . . . I tried to actually document what was going on, a truth, because it was all so terrifying, but
I could only capture a couple of seconds. With too much movement and people were running everywhere, the video became too dark, but we can still hear the panic . . .

TZ   I don't know how or why we remained when we all knew it took only 10 seconds for everything to be swept down by the lava. Why didn't we just leave? I know . . . but I keep on asking myself that
. . . . . .

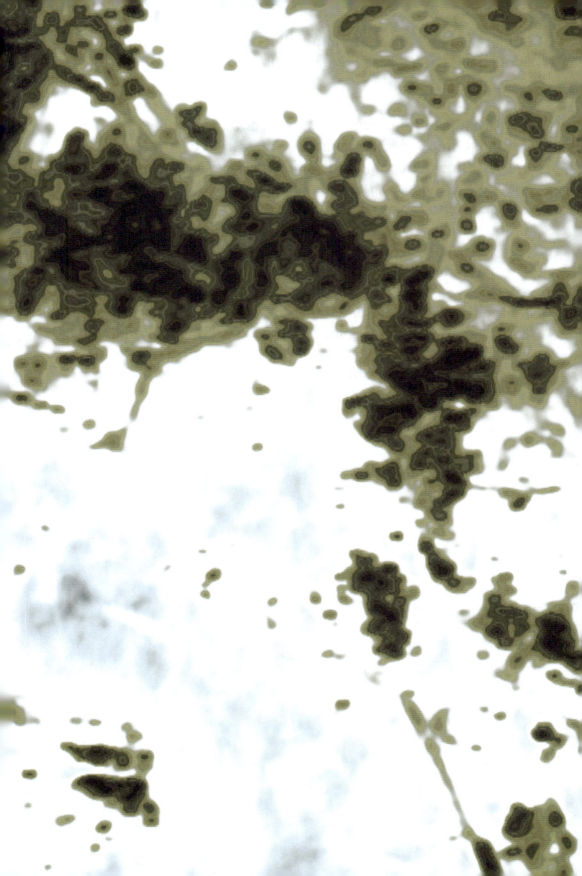

Sorry . . . I never meant to imply that . . . I just know it could have been worse if we were next to the lake.

. . . . . .

SN   What is left of documentation is edited, imagine if we just stopped editing images. I had tried for the longest time to document how people were living near that lake, either way, the measure of the carbon dioxide could not be visible. You could get punished for making it visible you know. That's why I left.

TZ   Yes, editing our images was like preparing for the afterlife, you know how our ancestors would prepare their grave? The makeup? Items to be buried with? Except that we did not want to be recognised, in the end, we had no image that looked like us, and mirrors had been removed a long time ago.

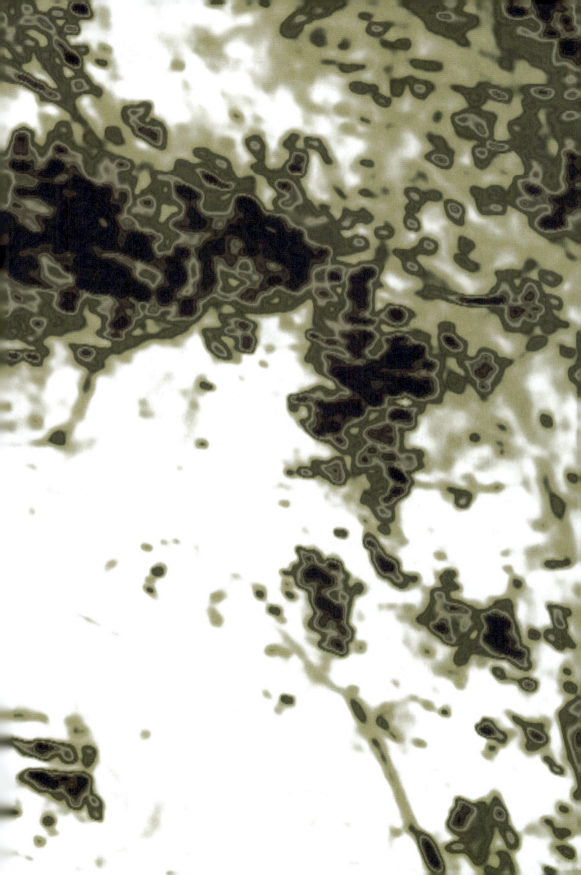

SN   My name is Solo Nkama, I am based in Mamugh. For the longest time I have worked with moving images but now I primarily work with text. I will talk more about this later . . .

I teach at Ehnjatenjate art school, and besides that, I like expanding my practice through working with other artists, I also curate shows and write for Wodmosam Magazine. A couple of years ago I curated a group show titled "You Are All You Need" in Ngogobeihli and I am currently working on a show that will open in a couple of months in Mamugh.

TZ   My name is Tala Zomi, I am an artist based in Ngogobeihli. I am primarily a sculptor and I also use text in my work. I started producing work that was inspired by closure, or thinking through and about closure. After what happened in Ngogobeihli, there was generally an interest in working through . . . and mourning the event by having exhibitions. I like to materialise my ideas through working with text, text as something physical—letters having a start and an end in themselves. Recently I have been working with books and publishing.

I, like many artists, spend a lot of time thinking about what it means to be an artist, or what it would be like for me. One of these overall methods I find interesting is hosting distortions. Doing that enabled me to generally take more risks.

What I find striking about your work is self-annihilation . . . ? For the longest time video was seen as the medium that would surpass us, having objects in the room seemed excessive.

SN   I remember the artist Didi Ongwanashi would basically exhibit their editing material, open, and

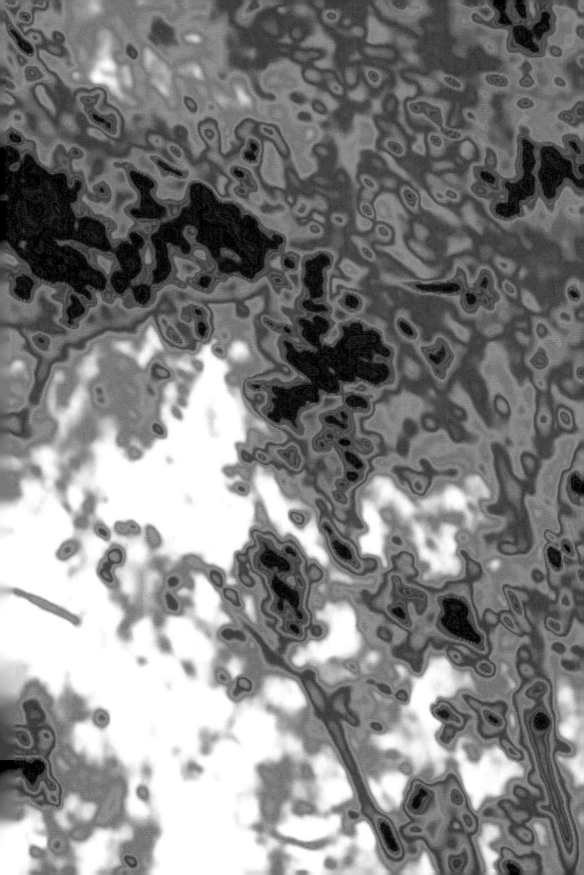

whoever came to the exhibition would be able to edit and even delete parts of the work that was there or do so later when they got home . . . So the work was being produced there and then and maybe, always just temporary? It seemed cheesy at the time, but the work was never meant to be finished. A work had to happen in a limited amount of time, and "disappear".

It was like we all agreed that video told lies, and the artist did not want to tell more lies.

TZ   Right? I remember it was almost like a panic, that unlike our ancestors, we were no longer interested in documenting a truth? With that work, the truth was not something fixed, the work was created there and then. Is that why you stopped working with moving images? You needed a truth? You were tired of telling lies?

SN   The last video I made was very short, very rich, like the volcanic soil it tried to capture . . . Still not convincing, or it does not show . . . I tried to actually document what was going on, a truth, because it was all so terrifying, but I could only capture a couple of seconds. With too much movement and people were running everywhere, the video became too dark, but we can still hear the panic . . .

TZ   I don't know how or why we remained when we all knew it took only 10 seconds for everything to be swept down by the lava. Why didn't we just leave? I know . . . but I keep on asking myself that.

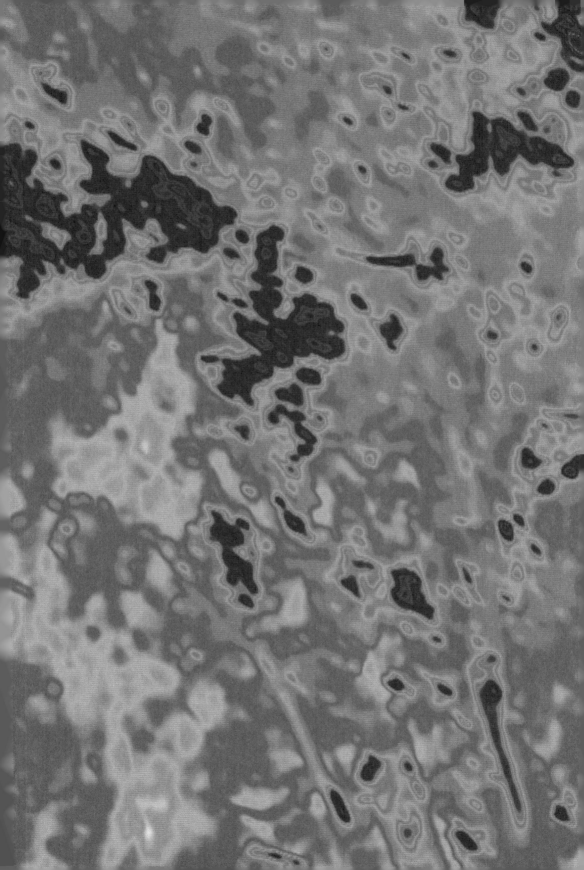

SN   My name is Solo Nkama, I am based in Mamugh. For the longest time I have worked with moving images but now I primarily work with text. I will talk more about this later . . .

I teach at Ehnjatenjate art school, and besides that, I like expanding my practice through working with other artists, I also curate shows and write for Wodmosam Magazine. A couple of years ago I curated a group show titled "You Are All You Need" in Ngogobeihli and I am currently working on a show that will open in a couple of months in Mamugh.

TZ   My name is Tala Zomi, I am an artist based in Ngogobeihli. I am primarily a sculptor and I also use text in my work. I started producing work that was inspired by closure, or thinking through and about closure. After what happened in Ngogobeihli, there was generally an interest in working through . . . and mourning the event by having exhibitions. I like to materialise my ideas through working with text, text as something physical—letters having a start and an end in themselves. Recently I have been working with books and publishing.

I, like many artists, spend a lot of time thinking about what it means to be an artist, or what it would be like for me. One of these overall methods I find interesting is hosting distortions. Doing that enabled me to generally take more risks.

What I find striking about your work is self-annihilation . . . ? For the longest time video was seen as the medium that would surpass us, having objects in the room seemed excessive.

SN   I remember the artist Didi Ongwanashi would basically exhibit their editing material, open, and

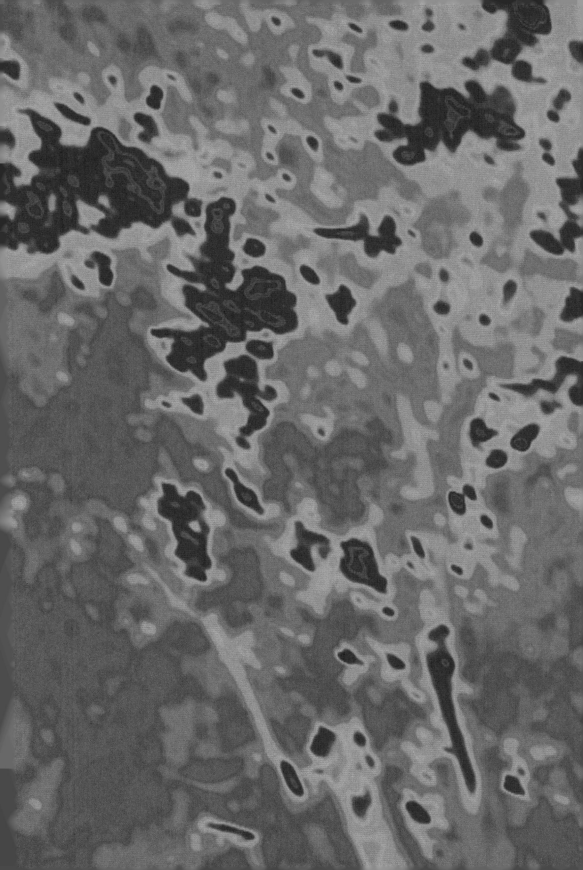

whoever came to the exhibition would be able to edit and even delete parts of the work that was there or do so later when they got home . . . So the work was being produced there and then and maybe, always just temporary? It seemed cheesy at the time, but the work was never meant to be finished. A work had to happen in a limited amount of time, and "disappear".

It was like we all agreed that video told lies, and the artist did not want to tell more lies.

TZ Right? I remember it was almost like a panic, that unlike our ancestors, we were no longer interested in documenting a truth? With that work, the truth was not something fixed, the work was created there and then. Is that why you stopped working with moving images? You needed a truth? You were tired of telling lies?

SN The last video I made was very short, very rich, like the volcanic soil it tried to capture . . . Still not convincing, or it does not show . . . I tried to actually document what was going on, a truth, because it was all so terrifying, but I could only capture a couple of seconds. With too much movement and people were running everywhere, the video became too dark, but we can still hear the panic . . .

TZ I don't know how or why we remained when we all knew it took only 10 seconds for everything to be swept down by the lava. Why didn't we just leave? I know . . . but I keep on asking myself that.
. . . . . .

Sorry . . . I never meant to imply that . . . I just know it could have been worse if we were next to the lake.
. . . . . .

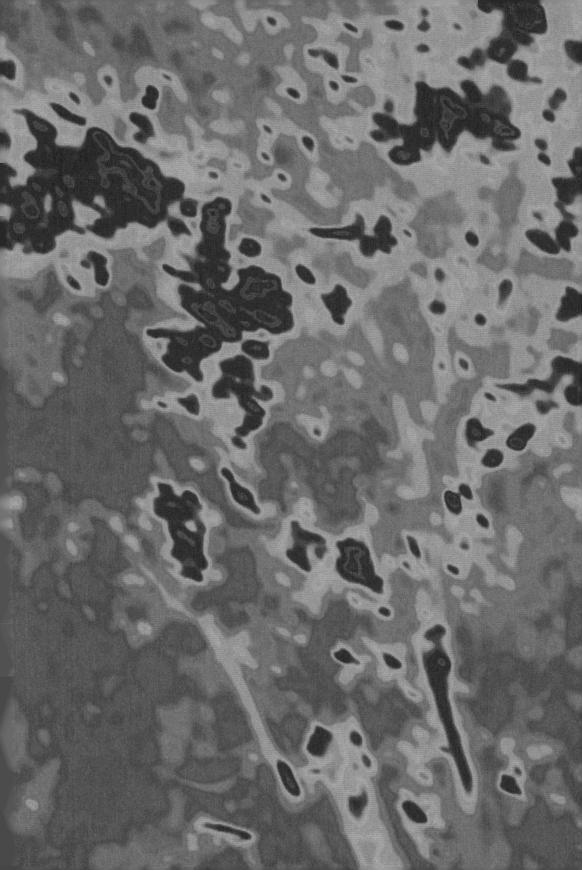

SN   What is left of documentation is edited, imagine if we just stopped editing images. I had tried for the longest time to document how people were living near that lake, either way, the measure of the carbon dioxide could not be visible. You could get punished for making it visible you know. That's why I left.

TZ   Yes, editing our images was like preparing for the afterlife, you know how our ancestors would prepare their grave? The makeup? Items to be buried with? Except that we did not want to be recognised, in the end, we had no image that looked like us, and mirrors had been removed a long time ago.

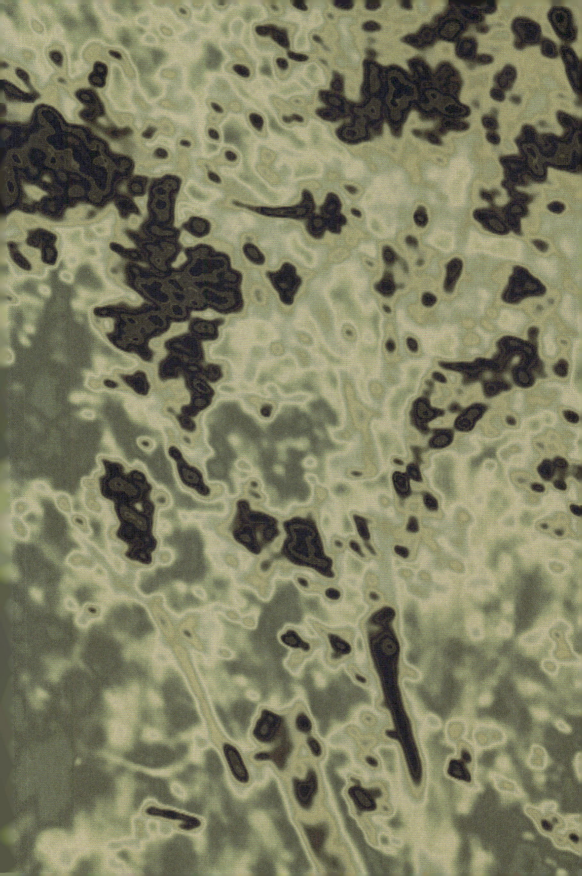

SN   My name is Solo Nkama, I am based in Mamugh. For the longest time I have worked with moving images but now I primarily work with text. I will talk more about this later...

I teach at Ehnjatenjate art school, and besides that, I like expanding my practice through working with other artists, I also curate shows and write for Wodmosam Magazine. A couple of years ago I curated a group show titled "You Are All You Need" in Ngogobeihli and I am currently working on a show that will open in a couple of months in Mamugh.

TZ   My name is Tala Zomi, I am an artist based in Ngogobeihli. I am primarily a sculptor and I also use text in my work. I started producing work that was inspired by closure, or thinking through and about closure. After what happened in Ngogobeihli, there was generally an interest in working through... and mourning the event by having exhibitions. I like to materialise my ideas through working with text, text as something physical—letters having a start and an end in themselves. Recently I have been working with books and publishing.

I, like many artists, spend a lot of time thinking about what it means to be an artist, or what it would be like for me. One of these overall methods I find interesting is hosting distortions. Doing that enabled me to generally take more risks.

What I find striking about your work is self-annihilation...? For the longest time video was seen as the medium that would surpass us, having objects in the room seemed excessive.

SN   I remember the artist Didi Ongwanashi would basically exhibit their editing material, open, and

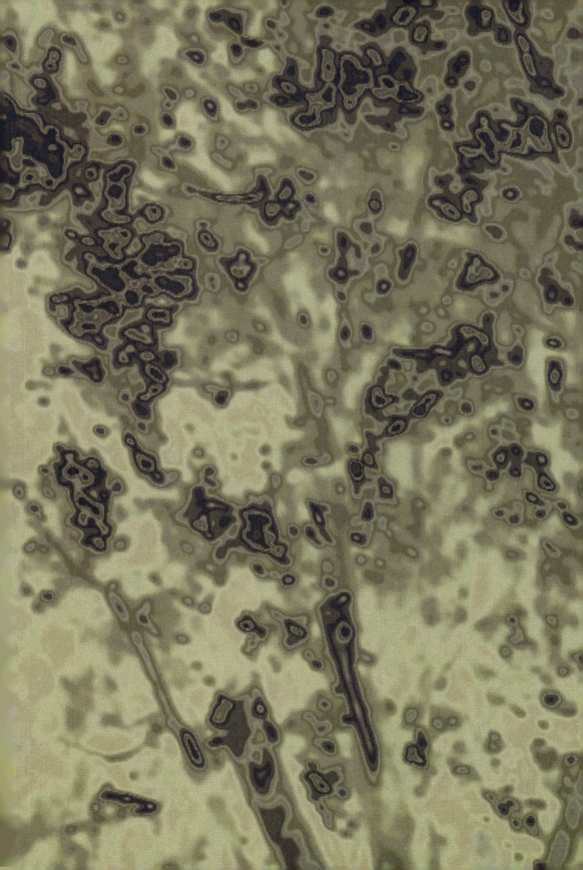

whoever came to the exhibition would be able to edit and even delete parts of the work that was there or do so later when they got home . . . So the work was being produced there and then and maybe, always just temporary? It seemed cheesy at the time, but the work was never meant to be finished. A work had to happen in a limited amount of time, and "disappear".

It was like we all agreed that video told lies, and the artist did not want to tell more lies.

TZ   Right? I remember it was almost like a panic, that unlike our ancestors, we were no longer interested in documenting a truth? With that work, the truth was not something fixed, the work was created there and then. Is that why you stopped working with moving images? You needed a truth? You were tired of telling lies?

SN   The last video I made was very short, very rich, like the volcanic soil it tried to capture . . . Still not convincing, or it does not show . . . I tried to actually document what was going on, a truth, because it was all so terrifying, but I could only capture a couple of seconds. With too much movement and people were running everywhere, the video became too dark, but we can still hear the panic . . .

TZ   I don't know how or why we remained when we all knew it took only 10 seconds for everything to be swept down by the lava. Why didn't we just leave? I know . . . but I keep on asking myself that.
. . . . . .

SN   The pools made me relaxed, maybe they functioned as a mirror too? Hehe, I was always so thirsty though, but all we could do was stare at it. That's all we did, we could not drink it. Maybe if it was boiled, but I was never

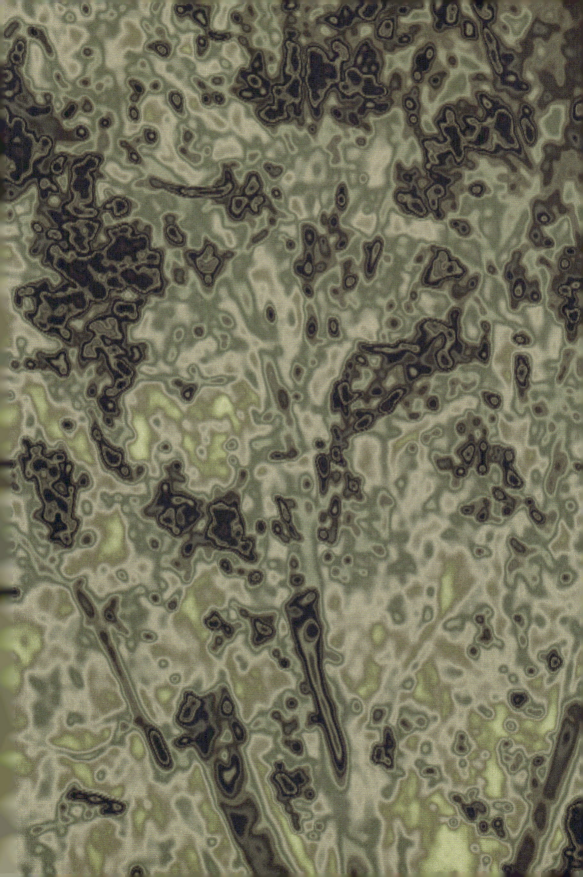

allowed near heat. The black pool calmed me down.
It calmed all of us down.

We were all so tired and stony, it became a difficult environment to work in. When we were in smaller groups, I would realise that I was not the only one thinking this. I think social media made people more "human".

TZ   Ja! Like when you would see the love a cold colleague had for their dog, or the same colleague posting a vulnerable love declaration to someone that could actually respond in a language we would all understand—we were all used to that though? It just stopped.

All of a sudden it became so embarrassing, I could meet this cold stony colleague you are describing here, and feel super sensitive. I would also hate that the thickness of my skin would get questioned in the form of gaslighting, instead of trying to understand the underlying violence that came from these spaces.

SINGING   *Amnesia amnesia, did you forget that I don't need ya—* such a great song.

TZ   My name is Tala Zomi, I am an artist based in Ngogobeihli. I am primarily a sculptor and I also use text in my work. I started producing work that was inspired by closure, or thinking through and about closure. After what happened in Ngogobeihli, there was generally an interest in working through . . . and mourning the event by having exhibitions. I like to materialise my ideas through working with text, text as something physical—letters having a start and an end in themselves. Recently I have been working with books and publishing.

SN   The eruption almost had an architectural spread and feel to it, still causing the ground to fracture . . .

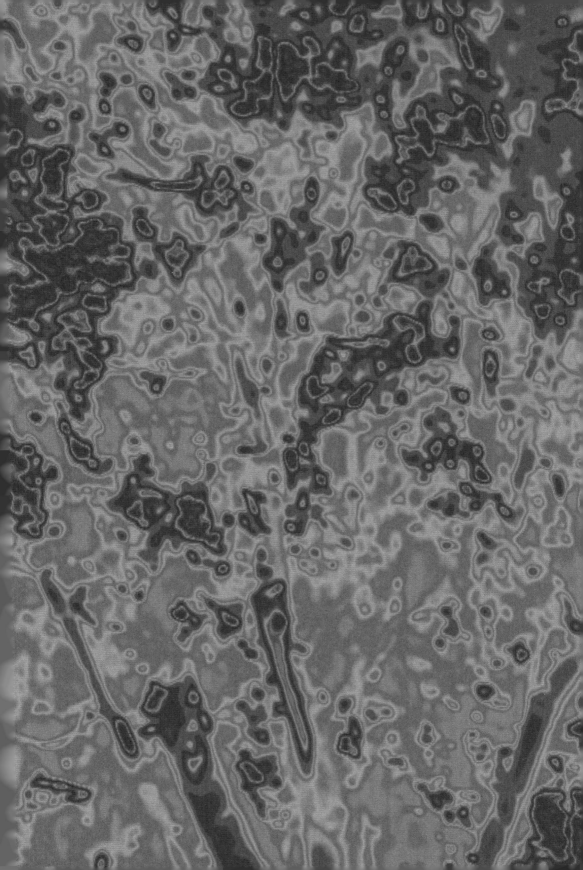

You know what, I remember there were dead flies everywhere because they were drawn to the light and when they came too close their wings would get burned and the heat would take them out.

. . .

SN   The disappearance has to be negotiated in relation to power, or an illusion of power. You know people would look at themselves as a martyr, as if there was no point for them to have a visible life if they merely existed to be consumed, they might as well disappear. To the forest. No one really knows what the forest is. My moods are so private, you know.

TZ   We don't have to talk about it.

SN   Like . . . am I fighting right now? Am I exhausted?

TZ   You know it's funny being here with you. I remember all these floods of science fiction films that came out. I would be like . . . Where are all the black people? Haha. Or where are we in this? Did we all disappear in the end? Did we disappear in the future? The screen became everything; if we did not exist there, we really did not exist.

SN   I think when you are not seen so often there is not so much space to doubt. It's like a friend whom you see every other year, there isn't so much space for them to show different sides of themselves. I decided to disappear under my terms, because I wanted to have a space to doubt, I couldn't doubt publicly because my body was already underestimated and sometimes overestimated for the wrong reasons. Since I couldn't doubt publicly, I couldn't really have a language for it. Like . . . Language needs to be exercised.

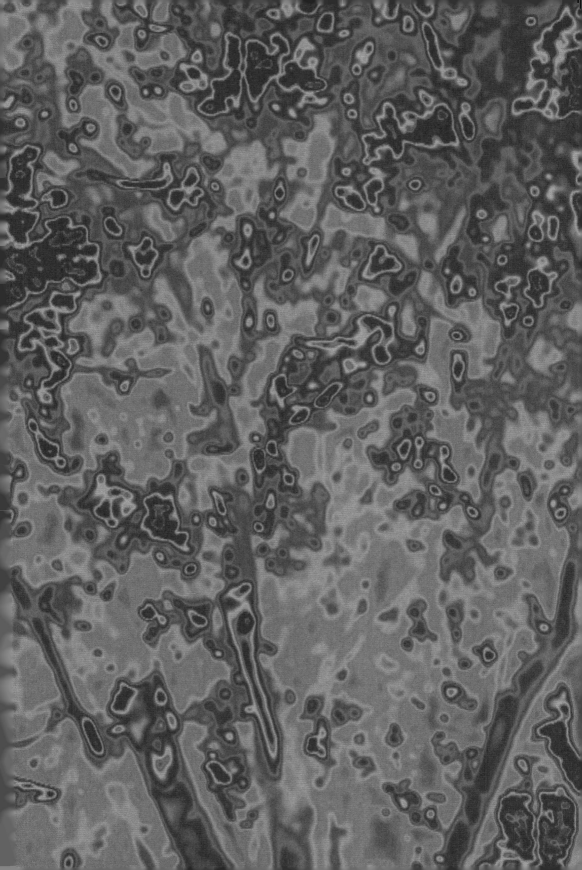

TZ   How to engage equity, how to engage historical responsibility?

SN   Ah I love that song! Yeah, I didn't really think I would be the one to run and hide. There just came a point where I just did not think it was worth it, being seen but not documented.

Let alone for a month, a week, a day, a minute? My body became heavier, and my body kept cleaning itself through sweat. [Puts her hands on her lower back and moves her arms]. What does pride have to do with it? Pride is a weakness, I heard.

TZ   Right? Because of the gaslighting, I would start questioning my sensitivity, and sanity.

How to discuss with someone when neither of those things is trusted.

I think we need to breathe.

Like seriously.

SN   Could it also be that I am continuously thinking about my potential, alternative versions of myself, I could have done this, I should have done this, but isn't that life? Us trying to find the best versions of ourselves in a given time? To survive?

TZ   You know the essay by Shnufaruko where we follow someone, not knowing which form they have for the outside world? They dive into the water, and when they come up they are no longer a fish, as I assumed, and now all of a sudden they can fly . . . Are they a bird? It becomes obvious how I continue to make this character smaller and smaller with my guesses.

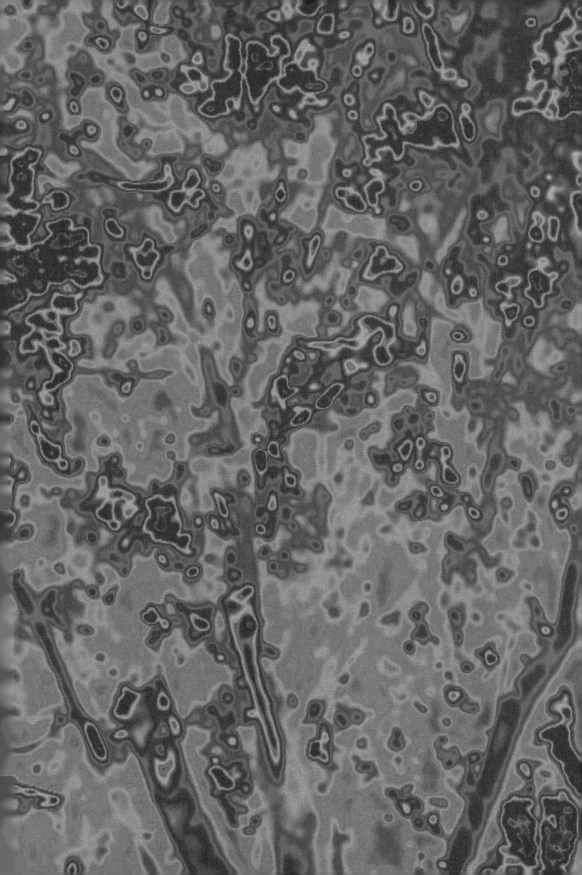

SN   Is that how it goes? I think I know which one you are talking about, but maybe I am remembering it wrong! Haha...

TZ   Distortion is fine, I have to be present for the distortions, and look at them as such. One of my favourite writers starts all their books from the dreams they have. So they have these intense dreams, and they continue to build the world when they wake up!

Remember we started with self-annihilation, maybe distortions could function as an echo of that.

For me, I saw a drastic shift towards self-annihilation. It all started with guilt, thinking of all the damage we had caused to other living beings—but at some point we were all trained in performing a guilt—there really wasn't that hesitation in saying sorry you know... remember when maybe as a kid you knew you were wrong but there was some part of you that really did not want to say sorry? But you could host that side of you and then say sorry... Like... Ok then... I'm sooooorry...

SN   The disappearance has to be negotiated in relation to power, or an illusion of power. You know people would look at themselves as a martyr, as if there was no point for them to have a visible life if they merely existed to be consumed, they might as well disappear. To the forest. No one really knows what the forest is.

TZ   Sometimes they would just look at me and say sorry, and I didn't even know where it came from. Like what had just happened...

It was just thrown around that word, sorry, and sometimes you really need the chance to say: Hey when you did this specific thing, that did not sit right with me.

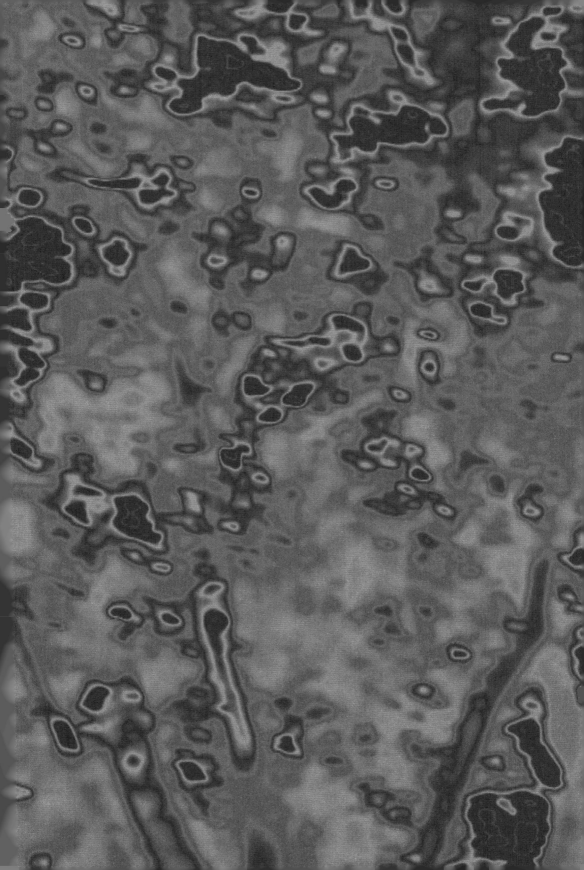

... And you could just not do that anymore.

SN   What are you saying? To be clear?

TZ   That they don't know what they are sorry about and I don't even know if sorry does anything for me.
SN   Oh I'm sorry ... [laughs]

TZ   Are you sorry?

You have spent too much time with yourself. You need something clear, a clear message, a clear breakthrough, you need to feel safe—if you feel safe, we will all feel safe. I am sorry you did not feel safe, you should have felt safe.

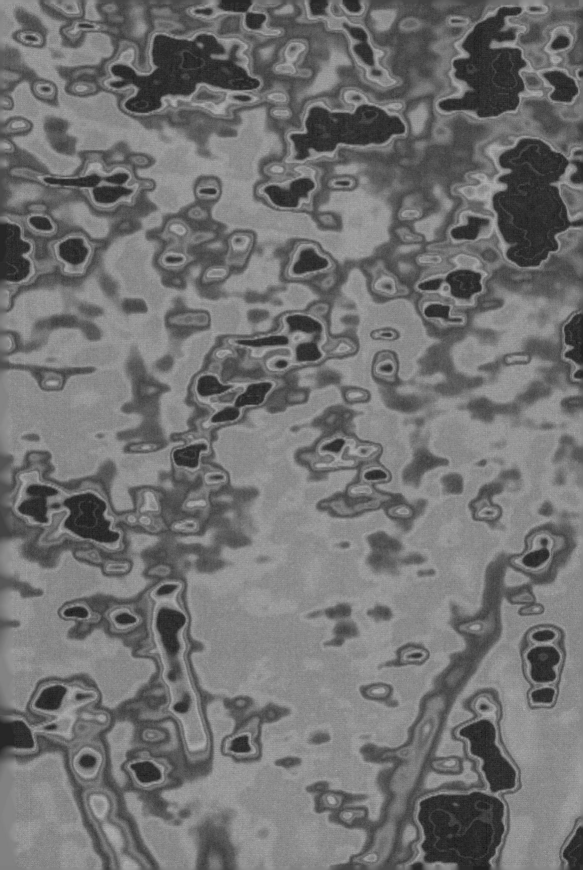

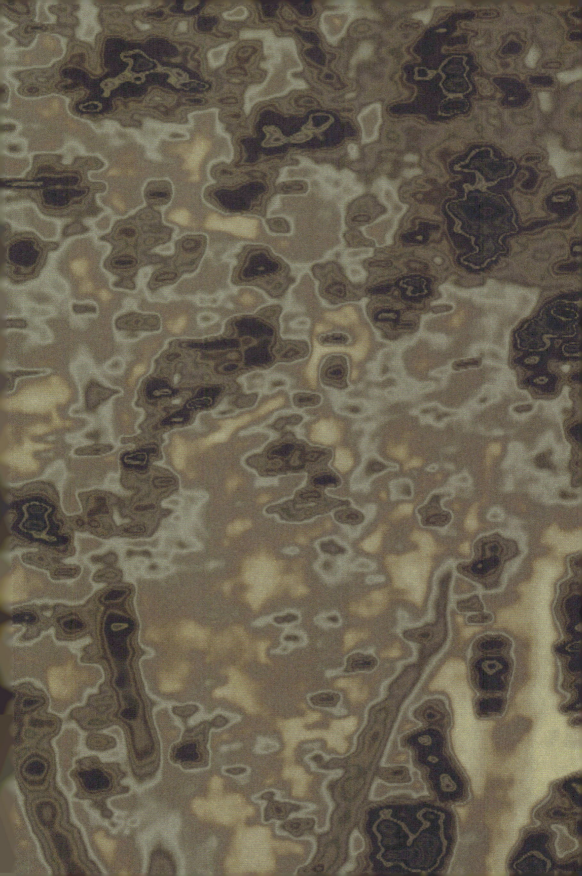

Re-Imagining Things III
Sandra Mujinga

1   [Talking to themselves] . . . Wait can I write that? What is happening in Kinshasa right now? I guess I can write back later, because my 4G is literally killing me right now.

2   You worry too much, just float with it.

1   I had this dream . . . I met Francine.

2   The Francine?

1   Yes, and in that dream she was hanging out with ranger Xaverine but she still made time for me and came up to say hi. It was dark, quiet and peaceful. We were all camping and there was enough food and medical supplies for all of us.

2   Wait a minute, isn't that an Instagram post you are describing? And the gorillas?

1   I know what you mean, but surely there is a reason that image exists?

2   What does this have to do with Kinshasa?

1   The gorillas remained hidden, I could only see their eyes in the dark.

Liiiikeee . . . We all thought it was corny to set up the fire, but Mwana Malamu and Bien Bien clearly demonstrated that they did not want to have ANYTHING to do with it.

2   Makes sense. Hey, they are young adults now. Still what does this have to do with Kinshasa?

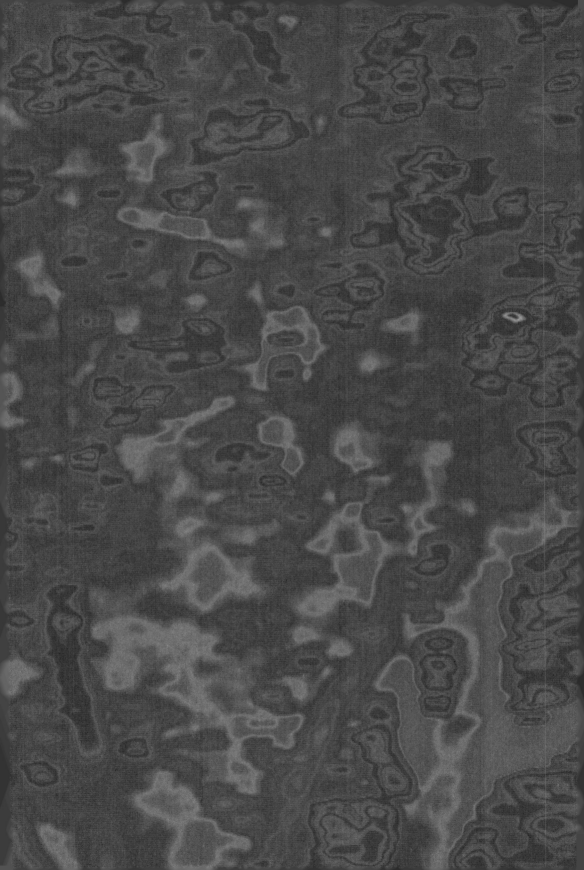

1   Yes they are, and they keep setting their boundaries like ... Mwana Malamu mimics Bien Bien. Aaaand ... Bien Bien is still not fond of me ... My tentacles were not even out, and surely I was reflecting my surroundings so I was visible.

2   Were you sitting close to the fire?

1   Yes, I can do that now. Can't you?

2   Were you not afraid of making it bigger?

1   That doesn't happen at night.

•

1   It feels like you think I am weaker than you, just because I am transparent. Just because I refuse to carry a skin.

3   Ummm okkkkk ...

1   Why can't you just say it? Admit it? There was a time, when we would all agree on one thing at least ... that underneath, the colour of the flesh was the same. Maroon, pink, purple and dark green.

3   I really have to go and collect some sticks now. I don't know what you want me to say?

1   I know that I carry a privilege, to actually choose. I know how my body goes well with ... can go through with ... Ok, can host echoes, and because of that I have been able to access my history more easily than you.

3   Yes?

1   That doesn't mean that I don't care. I am transparent but that doesn't really mean that you can see right through me. I am transparent but not made of glass. I am transparent, but protective of my inner flesh.

3   My back is reallllly itchy now, I really have to go.

•

2   Their voice sounds as if a wasp inhabits their throat.

1   How to re-imagine and not forget the future. How can critical theory exist on a practical level and not just as a beautiful painting on the wall?

2   If this is the apocalypse, what is next?

1   Sometimes I wonder if the bear knows . . . Knows that we are playing dead.

2   That word is not allowed to be used anymore.

They give the impression that, yes, they may have crossed the line.

But they would like us to use another word, since that word is too confusing.

To them.

That word does not mean anything anymore.

They say.

1   Not a transcendence. Not an escape. Not a resurrection.

But rather a saturation limited to, or in relation to his fantasy.

2   Some of us escape death, again and again.

And some of us relive it.

1   I was bitten by a snake and my skin keeps changing.

2   How many jellyfish do you actually know?

I love their culture, I have learned such and such a dance.

I feel special because I have so much knowledge about certain cultures.

1   I played that song so that I could cry.

2   I melted, or I boiled, I do not know. I just know I became soft, and I started to sweat.

1   The filters that are available hide, they function as a real mask should.

2   They travel to learn this specific rhythm . . .

1   You are brave because you love again and again . . .

2   You love again and again as if it was your job.

1   You love again and again as if it gave you super-powers.

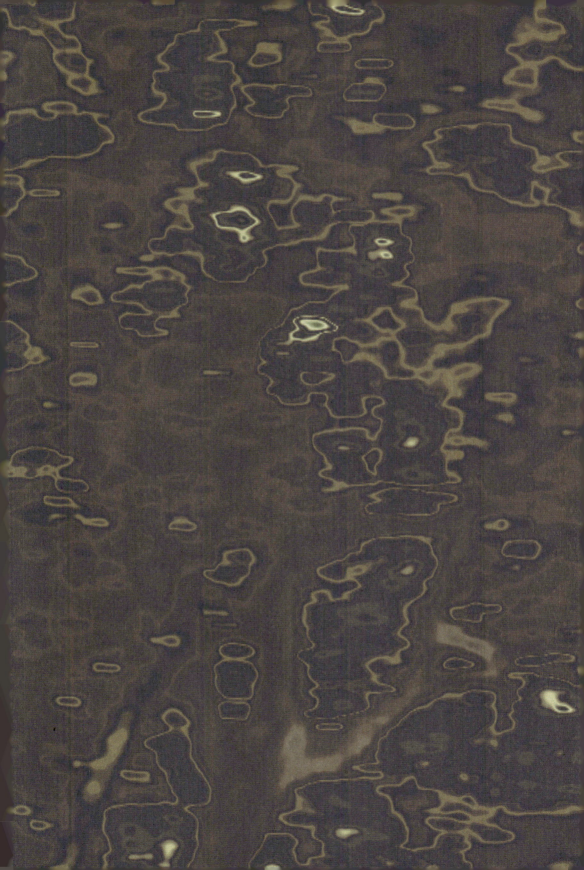

Colophon

Published by Bergen Kunsthall, Vleeshal, and BOM DIA BOA TARDE BOA NOITE on the occasion of the exhibitions:

Sandra Mujinga, "SONW – Shadow of New Worlds"
Bergen Kunsthall, 22 November 2019–19 January 2020
Curated by Steinar Sekkingstad and Axel Wieder

and

Sandra Mujinga, "Midnight"
Vleeshal, 20 September–13 December 2020
Curated by Roos Gortzak

Text: Wong Bing Hao, Tamar Clarke-Brown, Olamiju Fajemisin, Sandra Mujinga and Jessica Lauren Elizabeth Taylor
Visual essay: Sandra Mujinga
Editors: Roos Gortzak, Steinar Sekkingstad and Axel Wieder
Copy-Editing: Jasmine Hinks
Design: Studio Manuel Raeder
(Sylvia Lee and Manuel Raeder)
Printing: bud-Potsdam

This book was made possible with the support of Croy Nielsen, Vienna and The Approach, London.

The artist wants to thank all the contributors and a special thanks to Sjur Sævik.

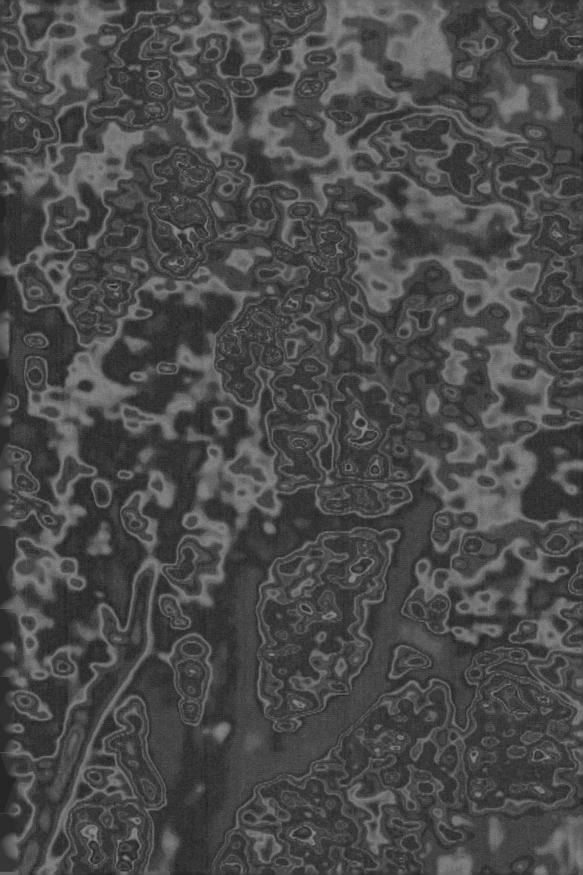

Olamiju Fajemisin, "There's Nothing Black About This", is a conversation with Sandra Mujinga conducted in Berlin on October 13, 2019.

Sandra Mujinga, "Amnesia? Amnesia?", is a script for a video installation, first presented at Noplace (Oslo, September 2019). Performed by Joe von Hutch.

Sandra Mujinga, "You Are All You Need", was first presented as a performance at Joinery LISTE in Basel (June 2019), upon an invitation from Spike Forum, and later at Bergen Kunsthall (November 2019). Performed by Terese Mungai-Foyn as Solo Nkama and Mariama Ndure as Tala Zomi.

Sandra Mujinga, "Re-Imagining Things III", was first presented as part of a three-day performance program at Sandra Mujinga's exhibition "Hoarse Globules" at UKS (Oslo, June 2018). Performed by Victoria Nunes Finstad and Sanyu Christine Nsubuga.

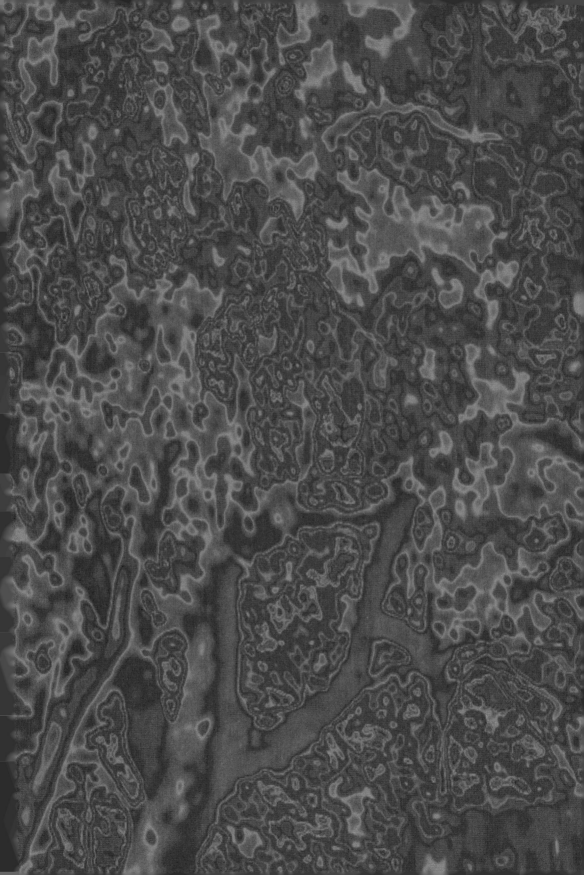

BERGEN KUNSTHALL

Rasmus Meyers allé 5
5015 Bergen, Norway
kunsthall.no

Director: Axel Wieder
Head of Finance and Administration: Maja Zahl
Programme Manager: Mai Lahn-Johannessen
Head of Education: Hilde Marie Pedersen
Curator Live Programme: Maria Rusinovskaya
Assistant Producer: Sofia Marie Hamnes
Curator: Steinar Sekkingstad
Techincal Manager: Jonas Skarmark
Gallery Manager: Einride Torvik
Head of Communications: Stein-Inge Århus
Reception and Tours: Dino Dikic, Åsne Eldøy, Sofia Marie Hamnes, Thea Haug, Ragna Haugstad, Andrea Grundt Johns, Caroline Larikka, Øystein Larssen, Tuva Mossin, Mia Øquist, Tord Øyen
Technical Team: Åsa Bjørndal, Åsne Eldøy, Robin Everett, Sarah Jost, Kristen Keegan, Dillan Marsh, Siv Torvik, Vegard Urne, Vegard Vindenes, Eric Alvin Wangel
Board: Espen Galtung Døsvig (Chair), Geir Haraldseth, Harald Victor Hove, Karen Kipphoff, Tom Stian Kosmo, Mai Lahn-Johannessen, Anne Helen Mydland, Hilde Marie Pedersen

BERGEN KUNSTHALL

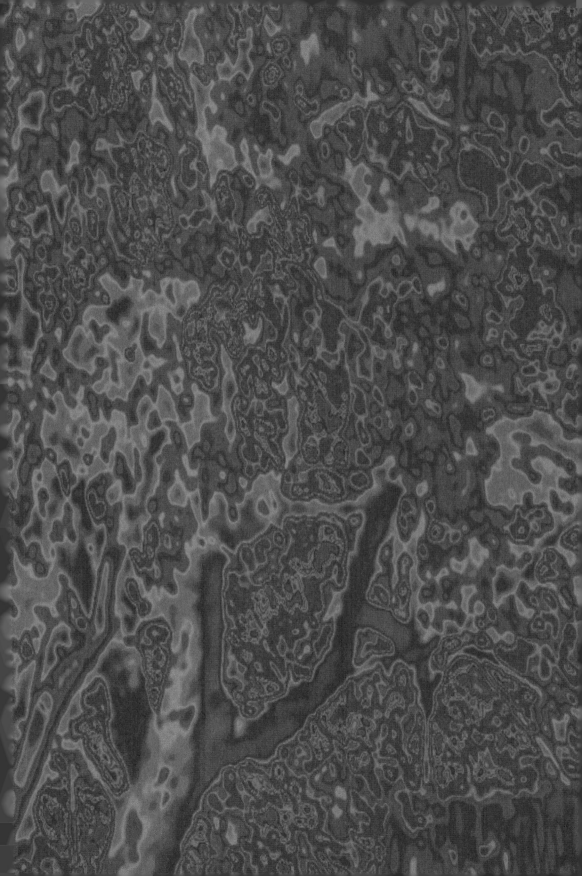

VLEESHAL

Helm 5
4331 CD, Middelburg, The Netherlands
vleeshal.nl

Director / Curator: Roos Gortzak
Management assistant: Hanna Verhulst
Curatorial assistant: Luuk Vulkers
Head technician: Kees Wijker
Hosts: Nicole Bianchet, Sien Christiaanse, Ruth Hengeveld, Zinzi Kok, Auke van Laar, Musoke Nalwoga, Suzan van de Ven, Dana Zoutman

Vleeshal

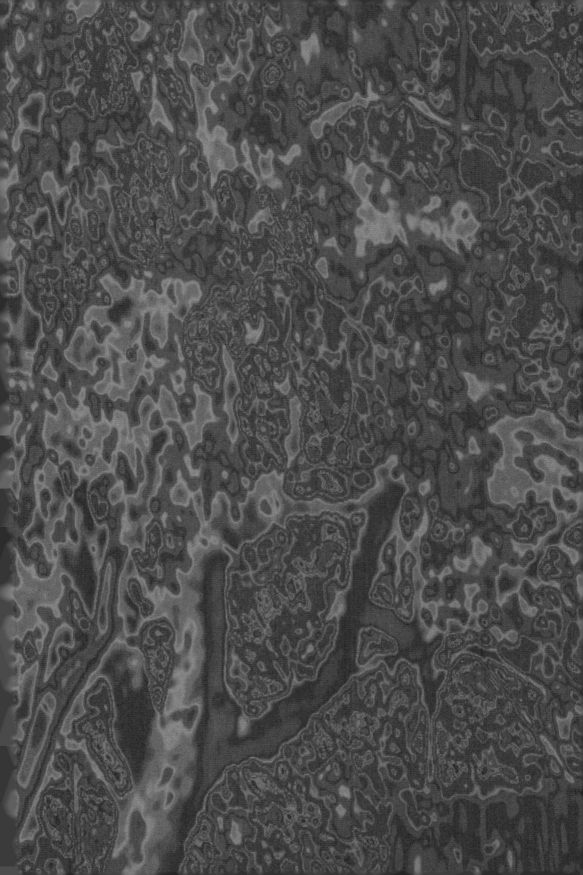

Published by

BOM
DIA
BOA
TARDE
BOA
NOITE

Rosa-Luxemburg-Strasse 17
10178 Berlin, Germany
www.bomdiabooks.de

ISBN: 978-3-96436-027-4

The Deutsche Nationalbibliothek lists this publication in the Deutsche Nationalbibliografie; detailed bibliographic data are available on the Internet at http://dnb.dnb.de.

All rights reserved. No part of this publication may be reproduced, stored in a retrieval system or transmitted in any form or by any means, electronic, mechanical, photocopying, recording or otherwise, without first seeking the written permission of the copyright holders and of the publishers.

© 2020 Sandra Mujinga, Bergen Kunsthall, Vleeshal, and BOM DIA BOA TARDE BOA NOITE

Printed in the EU

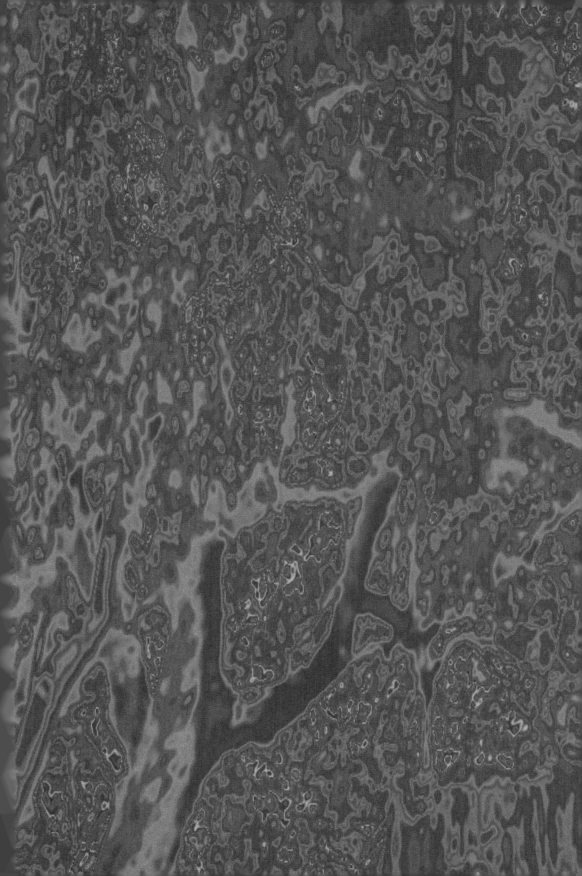